BURN FOR ME

EFFIE CAMPBELL

Copyright © 2024 by Effie Campbell

All rights reserved.

No part of this book may be reproduced in any form or by any electronic or mechanical means, including information storage and retrieval systems, without written permission from the author, except for the use of brief quotations in a book review.

For all those who love a wounded, morally grey hero who is obsessed with his woman...

...meet Phoenix

Ps. Sorry about the flare guns.

CONTENT WARNINGS

This book is written in British English, and set in Scotland and England. I use language and spellings from our fair isle rather than US spelling, so some words may differ slightly.

This is a dark romance book. It contains many spicy scenes, including praise/degradation. There is suspense, torture and violence, including erasing some (deserving) people from the world.

There are flashback/memory scenes which include death of siblings and other family members.

ONE

Laura

*P*reparing *to be a bride is exhausting. Even more so when you barely know the groom.*

The clipping of the gardener's shears outside the floor-to-ceiling window lined up with the thud of my footsteps as they hit the treadmill. Running had to be invented by the devil himself; I detested it. After my short but furious workout session, the mirror showed how red and shiny my face was, sweat dripping down and making me look like an overly oiled tomato.

The sun beamed into the home gym, adding more heat to my already melting body. I had to convince Daddy to get some blinds. Bill, the gardener, shuffled from one hedge to another as I tried to keep up some sort of pace. My lungs felt like they were going to explode, my pulse contributing to the cacophony of noise in my ears. Hitting the lower speed button, I gave in to defeat.

Three weeks to my wedding day wasn't enough to try to shave off the extra pounds I had. I didn't even care about them, really, but my mother sure did.

'Laura, should you be eating pasta?'

'Laura, look at the way your stomach bulges in those trousers.'

'Laura, have you come across this new diet?'

I tried to reason with her that Massimo had seen me in all my not-entirely slim glory, and he still wanted to marry me, but she was having none of it.

'There will be pictures, my dear. Pictures last forever.'

By twenty-six, I'd expected my life to have been a bit more exciting than sitting around waiting to marry the man my father chose for me. Thank god he was my type, at least. Tall, dark, and handsome, the classic trio. Massimo Ricci wouldn't have been out of place on the cover of one of those rippling ab magazines. By far, he's hotter than any of the guys I'd briefly dated at university. Other than those illicit dalliances, my parents kept me on a tight leash—and not even in a good way. My parents filled my days with dinner parties and events, gallery visits whenever another one of my mother's friends decided to pick up a paintbrush or have some other wealthy mid-life crisis.

A life of champagne and caviar wasn't so bad, but recently things had become more strained between my parents. While they hadn't exactly married for love, their relationship has always been easy. Mother hosted, Daddy worked. Elijah, my brother, and I followed them about in a suitably gendered manner. Elijah followed Daddy into business, while I spent my days with the same fake smile plastered on my face as my mother did.

Would it be any better becoming Massimo's wife? The letters he sent me every few weeks promised passion and desire, a marriage filled with excitement. Maybe I could finally put my degree to use by starting a business. I found it laughable that my brother would inherit everything, despite me having a business degree. At least, laughing spared me from crying about it.

I leaned my sweaty head against my hands, elbows resting on the treadmill's console, attempting to convince my pounding heart that it needn't burst out of my chest. After all, people exercised daily and lived to tell the tale. The wobble in my legs only added to my body's protest. It wasn't even like I disliked my body; a little softness felt good on me. However, my mother's dismay at being slimmer than me, at fifty and after having two children, was hard to ignore. She seemed oblivious to the fact that while Elijah took after her willowy appearance; I favoured my father. I inherited his overly large blue-green eyes and his pale English skin tone. Even our hair was the same mousy brown colour. No wonder Elijah was the golden child; he was her spitting image, with his blond hair and long legs.

What she despised the most was that I didn't hate myself. If I had, she'd at least have known I was suffering and striving to change, which would have validated her feelings about me.

But fuck her. Massimo was going to marry me as I was, and I would finally be free. I'd have my own home, my own allowance, and I'd be able to do whatever I wanted. I couldn't bloody wait.

After wiping off the equipment, I headed to my room, stopping by the kitchen to grab a bottle of water from the fridge. As I leaned back against the counter, it occurred to me

I had no idea what my new home with Massimo looked like. He wasn't one for social media, and he'd never sent pictures. According to my mother, he had a few homes, mostly in Southern Italy, but his primary residence was in London. That's where we'd begin our married life.

Sipping my ice-cold water, I glanced over the sleek expanse of my mother's kitchen. It was the heart of our home and was as perfect and controlled as she was. Hell, the entire house was like the inside of a brand-new fridge—all spotless, white and chrome. And cold. There wasn't an ounce of warmth or comfort. Everything shone, yet nothing made me feel any sense of belonging. We'd only moved into the new mansion two years ago, in a leafy suburb of Manchester. I'd wanted to stay in the south, near my friends, but Daddy had insisted we move. The house was bigger than our old one, but felt a million miles away from my old life. And far too sterile. A little colour would liven it right up.

'Oh, sweetie, you've been working out,' my mother said as she walked into the room, eyeing my red face. I focused on her and forced a smile. 'Good, good. This came for you.'

She thrust an envelope toward me, her eyes glittering at Massimo's neat, cursive writing on the front.

My pulse leapt all over again as my mind raced to what delicious words it might contain.

'Aren't you going to open it?' she asked, a little too eagerly, pressing a button on the coffee machine. It whirred into action, depositing a dark, heavily scented espresso into a petite white cup.

'After I shower, I'm sweating like a pig.'

'Laura Eloise Redgrave, you are a woman. You do not

sweat like a pig.' My mother's face hardened, and I struggled to hold back a laugh.

'So what do you call this?' I showed my sweat-stained t-shirt.

'Just a light sheen, sweetie.'

'Well, my light sheen and I are going to shower off. What are we doing for dinner tonight?'

My mother set one of her fake smiles on me and glazed over as though she was checking a mental diary of events. 'I have dinner with the girls from the country club. Daddy is out with Elijah on some business thing. You'll have to fend for yourself.'

I maintained enough decorum not to punch the air with my fist and say fuck yes.

'No problem,' I said as I took my water and my envelope and headed for the stairs in the large, open foyer.

'There's avocado and prawn salad in the refrigerator. You don't need to order anything in.' Her voice wafted after me, and I rolled my eyes. As if I was going to waste a night-in on my own on a fridge salad.

The crunch of mother's tires on the gravel driveway rose from outside as the evening sun cast luscious streaks of golden light through my windows. With spring newly abound, it felt like my life was unfurling like a new flower. The sweet scent of almond shampoo lingered in my freshly washed hair as I laid back on my bed, tearing into Massimo's letter.

My fingers trembled lightly while my eager eyes danced over the page. Biting my lip, I tried to savour the moment. I'd received a letter for each of the three months of our engagement, and with each one, my desire for my soon-to-be husband grew. After Daddy proposed the idea, it took weeks for me to agree to marry him. Dads didn't pick their daughters' partners in England, at least not since the Victorian era. I'd thought he'd gone bananas at the idea.

Until I met Massimo.

He towered over me, his dark hair sweeping over his tanned forehead. His words tinged with a deeply attractive Italian twang, and I'd practically wet my knickers on the spot. When he'd swept my hand up in his warm fingers and pressed a kiss to it, I'd made an illegible peep as my eyes bugged. Like my very own fairytale prince, he rescued me from my parents' overbearing tower.

It would have been perfect had I only got to spend more time with him ahead of the wedding itself. I hoped he wouldn't work as hard once we married. We had two weeks booked in paradise to get to know one another after the wedding, on his multi-million-pound yacht. Daddy had been on it once for a business meeting and told me all about it. The yacht had a chef and staff on call, and it had been decorated to the nines. I couldn't wait.

Finally, giving in, I read the letter. It was shorter than the others, but still left me squirming on the bed.

Sweetest Laura,

How I countdown the minutes until I can see you again. The last few weeks have felt like an eternity without another glimpse of your beautiful smile. My heart aches to hold you close, to run my fingers through your hair and feel your warmth against me. Night after night, I drift off to sleep with your gorgeous face filling my dreams and your name lingering on my lips. I long for the moment we can finally be together again, just you and me. How I suffer, my darling. Do you suffer as I do?

I cannot wait to wake up to the sweet melody of your voice every day, my love. To wrap you up against my chest and drink from your lips like a man desperate for the smallest taste of your divinity.

I count down the minutes, Laura.
Your love,
Massimo

My duvet squished beneath my bare feet as I wriggled on the bed, clutching the letter to my chest. Massimo was like something from my storybooks. A billionaire with dashing good looks and so utterly devoted to me already. I grinned up at my ceiling and pushed down the quiet whispers of doubt that crept up into my head.

You don't even know him.

Why would he want you?

It's a business deal.

Squeezing my eyes closed, I banished the niggles from my mind. No-one had demanded he send me letters. No-one had asked him to be so charming when we'd met. He'd been the perfect gentleman, engaged and interested. There were no red flags, so my brain needed to knock it off already. Not every guy was all Tinder dates and booty calls. He could be good without being too good to be true.

We could be happy.
We would be happy.
Together.

A note slipped from the envelope, a hardness in the middle of its folded centre. I opened it and stared. The golden credit card held my name on the front. Running my fingers over the raised lettering, I read through the briefer note.

> *A gift for you.*
> *Buy yourself whatever your heart desires.*
> *Clothing for our trip. Jewellery. Anything that makes you smile.*
> *There's no limit.*
> *M x*

I squealed as I sat up and read the note twice more. While my parents were wealthy, they kept Elijah and me on small stipends compared to our friends. To foster independence, so they said. But my fiance apparently had no such reservations. With absolute glee, I pulled up my phone's browser and immediately set to doing a bit of shopping therapy. My engagement ring sparkled in the last streaks of the evening light, sending dancing reflections across my thighs.

It reminded me that soon I'd no longer be the woman living at home under my parents' rule. No, the woman I was shopping for would be a wife to a very wealthy and adoring man. I needed clothing that said sophisticated and poise. Less English rose and far more European chic.

I had some research to do.

And some money to spend.

TWO

Phoenix

I was no stranger to blood and gore, but my stomach turned at the sheer amount of it as I walked into the elaborate dining room. Men lay where they had perished, blood oozing from every orifice in their tortured faces.

Stepping over a body, I glanced up through the glass eye pieces of my mask, the group of living people shifting awkwardly in the circles of my vision.

The tip-tap of blood and wine dripping from the dining table were the only sounds in the room, the air heavy with expectation. A bloated, putrefying body lay amongst the broken dishes, his arm hanging off the edge, almost outstretched toward me as if begging for help.

I hoped he deserved it.

I hoped they all did.

It wasn't my place to judge. Just to cover up the evidence with fire.

And I was good at remaining in my place. I'd learned it well enough.

I had three rules while under the employ of whomever required my unique services.

One: Burn it all. Two: Leave no witnesses. Three: Ask no questions.

It was always the same. I took the money and left them with nothing but flames and charcoal.

'What do you think?' Ewen McGowan, a member of Scotland's leading crime family, asked me. I tipped my head toward him and considered the job. The house was large, but suitably isolated. It would take a little while for the authorities to be called. I'd need to use more accelerant than usual and throw open the doors and windows, allowing the flames to rampage through the home like a herd of wild boars, ripping apart everything in their wake.

It was doable.

I loved a challenge.

I nodded once at Ewen. I'd worked with his family enough to know that he was good for the fee, and wouldn't give me any trouble paying it.

'How long?' he asked.

Flashing my hand four times to signal twenty minutes, I gave one more nod and left the small band of the living to see themselves out.

Navigating the luxurious country cottage, I opened every door and smashed through all the windows with my key's windscreen breaker, glass shards bouncing off my leather jacket. A fully prepared canvas always sped up the burning process and ensured thoroughness. As my uncle had often warned me, an ill-prepared man is set up to fail—one of the few useful nuggets amongst the beer swill and fists.

Shrugging my backpack down over my arms was a chore with my thick jacket, but eventually, I wrestled it to the floor and pulled out a jar of accelerant. My gas mask stifled the acrid scent rising from the jar, but from using it so often over the years, my mind filled in the missing information, and I scrunched up my nose anyway. Pulling on a set of latex gloves, I set about smearing the thick paste liberally around the home. I must have used half of the jar in the desecrated dining room alone. With all the bodies there, I had to be sure they went to nothing but blackened shards and pieces of bone by the time the police could get in after the fire had burned out.

Kicking a limp arm out of the way, I smeared the accelerant over the faces and fingertips of each body, ensuring the flames would gobble up the last vestiges of their humanity with fervour.

At last, the scene was set. A warmth seeped through my body as I pulled out a match and held it up in front of me. Such an insignificant little thing to cause so much chaos and destruction. Was there anything else in the world so small and simple that could wreak so much havoc?

Tingles crept through me as I placed the red head against the rough edge of the matchbox. With a shaky breath, I surveyed the room one last time. Everything was so still and quiet. If it weren't for all the blood, it could almost have been peaceful.

The scratch of the match head was the only sound before it crackled alight. Time slowed to nothing while I dropped it, watching as it crashed to the floor next to an unmoving leg.

Orange glittered and blossomed. Flames spread eagerly from that one point, licking at the body closest to it.

Adrenaline pumped as the room lit up. Fear. Memories. The reminder of the flames licking at my skin. I courted the pain for a moment before retreating. The fire was growing by the second, raging through the space and devouring everything within its path.

The fear has controlled me for so many years, but now I controlled it.

I am the flames' master. It does as I demand of it.

Yet, like so many beasts, if I didn't watch myself, it would happily consume me as readily as any other fuel.

I reached the front door and stepped outside, the house burned behind me, great orange flames cascading high into the dark night sky.

One of the group who'd hired me stood amongst the trees, a yellow glow flickering across his face as he watched me wide-mouthed.

I gave him one last nod before someone tugged him away through the trees.

I headed to my bike, waiting nearby, pausing for a moment beside it to admire my handiwork tearing through the building. I removed my mask and ran a hand through my sweat-slicked hair, allowing the cool night breeze and the warmth coming off the blaze to whisper over my naked face. Inhaling, my eyes close as I let the familiar sensation toy with me. A few moments later, I pulled on my lower face mask, covering everything below my eyes before sliding my helmet over my head.

With the flames lighting the surrounding area, I kicked my bike into action, the rev of the engine failing to compete with the terrific roar of the inferno behind me. The way the raging inferno danced in the chrome of my bike was mesmerising.

Reluctant to leave the glorious sight, I drove off into the night.

THREE

Laura

The zip slid neatly closed on my final suitcase, and I couldn't help but smile. Four sleek black cases, each with the designer's name embroidered on the front, stood at the end of my bed. Looking at them made me feel grown up and ready for the next chapter in my life. With polished nails, hair perfectly coiffed in waves over my shoulders, and a brand-new wardrobe suitable for a woman who belonged at his side, I'd liberally spent on Massimo's credit card to transform myself into his perfect wife.

Butterflies flitted in my stomach as I spotted the time. Only a few hours until Massimo arrived for the pre-wedding dinner. Mother had set it to be an intimate, family-only affair, with a bigger party to follow at the wedding venue later in the night. I wondered if he would kiss me. I hoped he would. Despite the tornado of nerves making my belly swim, I was ready to embrace my new life fully. The four cases held everything I was taking to my new home. Whatever was left was unneeded or replaceable.

Plopping down on the edge of my bed, I pulled Massimo's bundle of letters from one of the case's front pockets. I didn't even need to open them, though. I'd read them so many times I knew each one practically word for word. However, with each passing day, I realised more and more how much I enjoyed not only his words, but his attention. For the first time in forever, I felt desired, just as I was. Like someone out there had seen beauty in my many flaws and wanted me despite them. I only hoped his passion for me would remain stoked when we wed and began living together. I'd be on my best behaviour and try to instil all the etiquette my mother had pestered me with my whole life. Massimo deserved the very best wife, and he'd chosen me.

I wouldn't let him down.

Pulling off my leggings and hoodie, I slipped into a modest, yet pretty, dress that had cost an eye-watering amount. It was delicate and feminine, with soft layers of sheer white silk floating down from the fitted waist. As I topped up my lipstick with trembling fingers, I kept glancing at the wall clock through the full length mirror, half-wondering if it was faulty because time seemed to drag on so slowly. Drawing in a steeling breath, I finish the outfit with a set of understated pearl earrings my grandmother had left me. I'd treasured them for years as a lasting memento of her, and perhaps they'd be my lucky token as I ventured into my new life. In a way, she might even be there to guide me through it.

Inhaling deeply, I took one last glance at the reflection of a me I barely recognised in the mirror.

I bore a resemblance to my mother's friends' daughters,

who had already accomplished a lot in their roles as wives or career women. My abandoned leggings lay rumpled on the floor, like the shed skin of the person I was before Massimo.

Smoothing my skirt, I headed to the dining room.

My father leaned against the in-home bar, pouring himself a rather large whisky before reaching over for my brother's glass, topping it up.

'Hey,' I said, smiling awkwardly as both sets of eyes grazed over my appearance. 'I'll have one of those too, please.'

'Sure thing, kid.' Dad pulled a glass forward and dropped a generous measure into it.

'Still can't believe our little dumplin' has secured Massimo fuckin' Ricci,' Elijah said, his voice dripping with scorn.

I fucking detested the nickname he had always inflicted upon me. It had been a thing as long as I could remember. Little dumpling. Fat little pudding. My cheeks pricked with heat when he sipped his whisky with a smug grin.

'It's not my fault that not even Daddy can find someone who would marry you,' I replied, reaching past him to grab my glass.

Before I had the chance to take a swig of the fiery liquid, my mother plucked the glass clean out of my fingers and replaced it with a long-stemmed champagne glass.

'Don't use that tone with your brother. No one likes a bitter woman, Laura.' My mother handed the whisky glass over to my father and gave me a look of displeasure.

'He called me—'

'I don't care what he called you. It's your job to be sweet, darling, not right.'

I sipped at the extra-dry champagne and tried not to pull a face. At least it was alcohol.

'George, please don't give her whisky. Massimo doesn't need to come in here and smell that foul stuff on her breath.' My father shrugged and drank down the whisky in question. Elijah took a sip of his while holding my gaze, smacking his lips in a dramatic display of delight.

Rolling my eyes, I made my way to the window that overlooked our driveway. The sooner I got out of here, the better.

If only time could go faster.

Massimo Ricci was in my house.

Holy shit.

My skin was sticky as I tried to hold my body still in one spot. I fought the urge to pace as I heard the accented timber of his voice in the hallway. Using my hand to fan my fiery face, I pleaded with the gods to return my heart rate to a human level. I feared it would burst straight from my chest and land at my fiance's feet as he graced the room.

After a few moments, that felt an awful lot like a million years, the dining-room door opened at last.

'Laura!' Massimo's beautiful face broke into a grin as soon as his eyes roved over me.

I didn't know whether to kiss him or fucking curtsy. My body felt like jelly stuffed into a sausage casing as I awkwardly made my way toward him.

'Massimo, it's so lovely to see you again.' Stretching up on my tiptoes, I placed a kiss on his cheek, just left of his mouth. His body tensed as I did. Was he as affected as I?

'Indeed,' he said, giving me a tight smile before turning away as my mother and father walked in behind him.

'Shall we get dinner started?' my mother said. 'The chef has prepared us quite the feast.'

When I tried to take a seat next to Massimo, my mother tutted and directed me to one on the far side of the table, putting my brother and father next to my intended instead.

'Mum,' I hissed under my breath, 'Surely I should sit next to my soon-to-be-husband?'

'You've already secured your part of the deal, Sweetie. All you need to do is say I do and spread those thighs for him. Your brother and father still have potential connections to make.' She brushed past me, a fake smile plastered on her face as always.

Fury made my cheeks flame as I took my seat, idle chatter bubbling between the men while the entrees were served.

Massimo looked almost regal next to my brother. He sat straighter and spoke with a calculated ease. He was also just as handsome as I remembered. Imagining myself wrapped up in his toned arms in less than twenty-four hours had me near writhing in my spot. Would he be romantic and gentle with me? Or would he be passionate? Would he push me to my knees and...

Jesus, Laura. Not with your family in the room.

I shifted my focus back to the babble of conversation. The words were far more heated than I'd been expecting as I tuned in.

'You see, George, we had a deal, but it turns out that you

have been lying to me for months,' Massimo said, his eyes glittering dangerously.

My mother's eyebrows creased as she tried to follow the exchange.

'It's not like that.' My father's voice was strained, high-pitched and laced with fear. 'There were a few snags.'

'You call losing your connections through Belgium a fucking snag?' Massimo snarled, 'We had a deal. I marry your daughter, and you ensure the smooth passage of goods via the Belgian port.'

I'd known there was a business agreement behind our union, but to have it so blatantly said in front of me was like being punched in the gut.

No, I told myself, *his letters showed how he really feels.*

'And worse than that, I find out you and your son have been undercutting me for months. Taking my stock and selling it out beneath me while pretending everything's been fine. Did you think I wouldn't fucking find out?' Massimo's face had twisted into a truly frightening mask. Anger replaced any sign of the man I'd briefly met before.

'George,' my mother gasped. 'Is this true?'

Elijah rolled his eyes. 'Don't act as if you didn't know, mother. It was your idea.'

My brain felt like it was seeping out of my ears as I looked from one face to another. They had all been lying to my fiance and me for months? They'd undercut him in business? What the hell?

My head pounded as I stood, a wave of nausea sweeping over me.

'I need to use the bathroom,' I blurted out, heading for the door.

'It's too late for talk,' Massimo continued, talking over whatever my father was saying. 'There is no room for rats.'

An ear-splitting bang rang out behind me. I whipped my head around to see a large spray of red across the wall behind where my mother sat. She slumped over into her venison, gravy dripping down her front and mingling with the blood flowing from the hole in her head.

A scream tore from my throat, and another gunshot cracked like thunder.

I needed to get to my phone, but I'd already packed it in my case. Kicking off my heels, I raced toward the kitchen, hoping to send the chef to get help.

Chef was laying in a pool of crimson.

Backing out of the room, I dashed for the doors. I needed to get out. My feet slid on the tiled flooring as I raced for the door, but two men were visible through the frosted glass, guarding the exit.

Fuck.

A third shot cracked, and I crashed up the stairs, my heart beating as hard as my feet against the wood. Sobs wracking my body. Footsteps crashed behind me, and I glanced over my shoulder as I reached the top of the stairs. Massimo pursued, gaining on me. A bullet splintered the wall behind my head as I careened toward my bedroom.

Slamming the door closed, I locked it and grabbed my phone from my bag before going into the bathroom and locking that door, too.

My hands shook as I pressed my finger against the on button, waiting for my phone to kick into life. I heard my bedroom door crash open and Massimo tearing open my cupboards.

'Come on,' I pleaded with my phone. 'Please?'

A loud kick made the bathroom door shudder and tore another startled scream from my throat. At last, my phone's home screen lit up. I hastily punched in nine-nine-nine, my fingers slipping in my frantic rush to summon help.

The door gave way and Massimo burst into the room, a dark gun pointed directly at my forehead. Tears blurred my vision as I compressed myself back into the corner.

'P-please,' I choked on a sob.

Reaching down, he snatched the phone from my hand and hung up the call before dropping it to the floor and crashing his heel down on top of it.

'Please, Massimo. I had no idea.'

His breathing was hoarse as he let out a laugh. 'I don't doubt that.'

'Don't hurt me.'

'I don't have a choice. Your family is dead. I can hardly marry you tomorrow without raising some serious questions, can I?' Blood speckled his tanned skin, and the realisation that they were all dead hit me like a tonne-weight.

'I thought you loved me,' I whispered as he ran a hand through his blood-slicked hair.

'I don't even know you.'

'But the letters...'

He laughed again before shaking his head. 'Do you think I have time for penning love letters to stupid little English girls? Your mother arranged them to keep you sweet.'

'Don't kill me,' I begged, tears washing down over my cheeks. I'd gone from the promise of everything to pleading for my life in what felt like a matter of minutes. 'Please, I'll do anything.'

'You hardly had anything I wanted, even with everything your father offered me. Without it, you're barely worth the bullet.'

Before I could take a breath, pain bloomed in my chest as my ears rattled with the sound of the gunshot. Looking down, my pretty white dress had a hole above my left breast, red petals of blood growing out from the torn point.

'Massimo,' I whispered.

He was already gone by the time I hit the floor.

FOUR

Phoenix

I'd barely made it twenty miles along the motorway when a buzzing started in my pocket. With a groan, I pulled my bike over in the lay-by and tore my leather gloves off.

The screen lit up with a number I didn't recognise.

Ignoring it was tempting. I could be back on the boat and tucked up in bed within the hour if I headed straight for the dock. My ass ached from the hours I'd spent on my bike throughout the day, and my clothes reeked of smoke. A hot shower called out to me like a siren.

Yet, the buzzing didn't stop, and curiosity got the better of me.

Clicking the green symbol, I hauled off my helmet and pressed the phone to my ear.

'Is that... Phoenix?' A man's voice said on the other end of the line, his words slow and hesitant.

I waited. If he knew who I was, he wouldn't truly expect an answer.

'I've got an urgent job that needs taking care of. In Manchester. Entire house needs to go up and fast. Four bodies with gun-shot wounds. I'm more than happy to pay your going rate.'

Closing my eyes, I inhaled through my nose. Every part of my body screamed to say no, to curl up in bed. I didn't need the money, and I'd already had my fix of destruction.

But there was a kernel of burning need awakening deep in my soul. A need to please. A need to be useful. A need to not be alone again.

So many days stretched out, filled with nothing but me and the expanse of the ocean.

What was one more job?

I promptly hung up and ignored the call that had rung almost immediately after.

Pulling up a text, I set out my terms.

> I need the address. How much time has elapsed since the incident?

A light rain kicked up, sending a sheen of tiny raindrops scattering over my phone screen.

> Twenty minutes. Oak Grange Manor. I'll send a pin that should get you directly to it.

> £100K

The reply bubbles danced for a few minutes as I waited.

> That's double the fee I was told.

> You can take it or leave it. I was about to head home.

Another full minute of waiting.

> Fine. But make sure it's thorough.

> I'll need a name, and for the wire to clear by the time I get there.

> Why do you need my name?

> Insurance. Just in case anything should happen to me.

Working for someone new who could afford my services and had a habit of killing people was always a risk. Being implicated on either side of a war could prove positively fatal. I wanted to keep breathing, despite my better judgement.

Being dead might well be better than the life I lived.

I'd been cheating death for longer than I deserved. Some day, he'd catch up.

The game was how long I could outrun him.

My phone buzzed once more.

> Massimo Ricci

The wire transfer for one hundred thousand pounds arrived as I fitted my helmet back over my mask. Good thing I always travelled with extra supplies.

T wo muscle-clad heavies stood by the front doors of the pretty, if soulless-looking, new-built mansion. The driveway and surrounding lawns were almost too perfect. Not a single blade of grass dared stand out of place. Cold air whispered over my ass where I'd grown sweaty against the bike. The journey had me wiped before I'd even started the job.

Balancing my helmet on the saddle of my bike, I ran a hand through my sticky hair and down over my masked lower face. My skin itched to feel the cold air on it, but it wouldn't happen until I was back safe on my boat, miles from civilisation.

One man came towards me as I pulled my gas mask and supplies from my backpack.

When I glanced up at him, he startled, before coming to a halt.

'Mister Ricci is inside.'

I nodded once before continuing to prepare for the incoming blaze.

My gas mask fitted neatly over my face, and I pulled the rear straps until it fit tightly against my skin, making a seal to protect me from the destruction I brought.

Massimo Ricci lounged back on a dining room chair, his feet up on the table while he sipped at a cup of tea.

He didn't look up when I walked into the room, just kept on drinking.

The wall to my left was awash with sopping pink globs of

brain and bright red droplets of blood. A blonde woman lay slumped forward on the table, a crimson puddle leaking from her concealed face and spread out halfway across the table. Massimo's shiny black shoes sat crossed just beyond where the red trail ended.

A younger adult male's body hung off of another ornate dining chair, his skull half caved in at the temple.

The one I presumed to be the head of the family—a squat, mousey, brown-haired fellow—had made it almost out of the dining room before being taken out. His fingers remained clenched around the stock of his gun. He'd tried to fight for his family, at least.

Massimo had said four bodies.

Looking around, I failed to spot the fourth.

'Last one's upstairs,' Massimo said, standing and finally setting his stony stare on me. 'I trust you'll make sure no-one can tell what happened here?'

I gave him a nod.

I knew perfectly well how to do my job. People didn't hand over wads of cash to an amateur.

'Right. Well, I need to head off to my engagement party and make it appear as if my fiancee stood me up.' My skin bristled at the unwelcome touch. Clenching my hand into a fist, I waited for the front door to close behind him.

The three of them climbed into a black car and drove slowly down the long, winding driveway.

The home's interior was like a mausoleum. Everything was solid white, bar the great red sprays of blood that decorated the dining room. Hitting a light switch did nothing. The power was cut. Likely Massimo's crew to disable any cameras or alarms.

Saved me a job. I didn't need built-in smoke alarms to bring the fire crews too quickly.

Working methodically, I spread the accelerant through the home, opening the windows and doors while humming softly to myself. I always hummed when no-one was around, hoping the muffled noises might stop my vocal chords from atrophying from lack of use.

Not that I'd likely ever need them again.

Taking the stairs, I worked the accelerant up their glossy wooden bannisters, heading into room after plush room.

Clothes lay crumpled on the floor in one room, while another was perfectly neat. Expensive creams and perfumes lined the counters in an adjoining bathroom, while designer clothes stocked the walk-in wardrobe.

The waste always pained me.

Taking anything would provide a solid lead back to me, so I stuck to the plan.

Prepare. Burn. Leave.

A perfect plan that, in over a decade of working for myself, had never failed me.

Only one room was left on the upper floor, and I walked in, wondering if the final body Massimo had mentioned would be there. The room was feminine and pretty, with matching cases lined up at the foot of the bed. I guessed their owners' vacation had been cut real short.

Humming a tune I only vaguely recollected from my childhood, I worked the almost empty pot of accelerant over the furnishings.

An internal door in the room remained ajar, so I pushed it open with my boot. A bare foot greeted me. Along with a red puddle.

Sighing, I stepped into the bathroom. A beautiful woman sat slumped back against the wall, a bloody wound on her chest. Crouching down, I looked into her pretty face.

The accelerant squelched between my gloved fingers as I reached forward and spread some across her forehead.

A whispered groan escaped her lips, and I fell backward, almost shitting myself in surprise.

Holy fuck.

She was alive.

Backing up, I stared at her. Her face was pale, and her elegant white dress was stained with a streak of red down the front. Dark lashes flickered against her cheeks, and my breath caught within my mask as she opened her eyes.

Despite being unfocused, they were like great pools as big and deep as the ocean itself. I'd never seen eyes quite like them. Almost too big for her face, overriding her other features.

My pulse quickened when her gaze focused on me.

'Please, help me,' she whispered in a hoarse tumble of words.

Leave no witnesses.

Leave no fucking witnesses.

She was as good as dead, anyway. Burning her in the home wouldn't make a difference.

Right?

Standing up, I stepped back right as she reached out for me. Her blood-stained fingers grazed my thigh, and I sprung back as her touch seemed to burn through to my skin.

'Please, don't leave me,' she sobbed, her voice catching. A trail of wetness cascaded down her cheek, and the urge to touch the salty stream made me clench my fingers.

I wanted to take her.

No-one would know. She'd be a ghost, like me.

If she didn't die.

Shaking my head, I ruled out the insane idea. They'd expect a fourth body, and no matter how well I incinerated the home, they'd eventually discover a missing skeleton. Bones didn't burn well.

I resumed humming while spreading the remaining accelerant around her, her sweet sobs harmonising with my tune.

'Come back for me.' Her rasping voice reached me as I stepped out of the bathroom. 'Please?'

The words immediately transported me back in time. She wasn't the first to ask this of me, but the last time someone did, I had promised to help—and then broke that promise.

This time, I walked away without looking back.

You couldn't break a promise you never made.

FIVE

Laura

His footprints faded as the seconds ticked by, and despair welled up in my chest.

But I was alive.

Maybe my family survived too. I had to find out.

An acrid smell assaulted my nose, and I scraped my fingers across my face, gathering the goop the man had smeared on me, trying to figure out what it was.

My stomach churned as I heard him moving around the next room, wondering if it was one of Massimo's men or if he'd actually come back for me.

An old-fashioned-looking gas mask had obscured his face, painted with a worn, fiery bird across the forehead. He didn't look like one of Massimo's sharply attired henchmen.

Excruciating pain shot through me as I struggled to shift. With a weak groan, I forced myself to sit upright while my muscles trembled with effort. My vision swam, and I blinked hard to clear it. That was when I saw it—beneath the ripped white dress, there was a red-glazed hole in my chest.

Fuck.

Massimo shot me.

He fucking shot me.

Pain flooded my senses as I pressed my hand to the floor and pushed myself forward an inch. I had to get out.

Tears wet my cheeks with every tiny movement, the searing sensation in my chest winding me.

Unless Massimo had caught a lung.

No, Laura, stop. One thing at a time. Get out.

I hauled myself to my bedroom, thick black smoke creeping in through my doorway.

'No,' I whispered, panic rising.

I needed to move faster.

But my body was weak, exhaustion making my limbs uncooperative. I'd lost too much blood. It caked my torso, seeped between my fingers, and pooled around my thighs on the bathroom floor. Still, it leaked from my chest as I dragged myself forward, leaving a trail behind me.

The air in the room grew hot and thick, making my lungs ache with every breath.

The carpet grazed at my knees with each of my shuddering movements.

Bright orange flames hurried around my door frame, eagerly dancing their way into my room.

Smoke stung at my eyes, and I swiftly diverted my slow course towards one of the open windows. Through quivering sobs, I swallowed down a scream as I weakly grabbed the window frame and propelled myself forward, desperate to draw in the cool, fresh air.

Looking down, I realised the only way out was to throw myself onto the tarmac below.

My entire body protested as I pressed the flesh of my palms into the window sill and hoisted myself up onto the edge.

I was ready to jump when I caught a flicker of movement at the edge of my vision. The masked man was swinging a leg over a motorbike and kicking it into gear..

'Please, help me,' I called, my voice lost over the roar of the growing fire.

A cry rang out, and Bill raced toward the bike, brandishing a huge set of gardening shears.

No.

Bill, hide.

But it was too late. The masked man swerved, his bike skidding out from beneath him. Bill rushed him, the shears open wide.

Sweat dampened my back from the inferno behind me, as I watched the masked man fight him off.

The crack of Bill's neck echoed loud enough for me to make it out over the fire, the masked man's hands jutting his neck harshly to the right. His body crumpled to the ground. A gasp tore from me, my bloody hand coming up to my mouth.

The man humphed Bill over his shoulder before looking back at the house, his eyes seemingly meeting mine through the circular windows of his mask. He carried Bill as easily as if he were a child, his thick arm slung around Bill's limp thighs.

He came back into the house.

Fear warred with hope.

There were only two options; he'd save me or kill me.

My room was half ablaze, my suitcases melting as the fire greedily devoured them.

Massimo's letters curled and blackened on my bed, my mother's false words burning away by the second. The window beckoned me. If I didn't survive the fall, I could only hope it would be a quicker death than being burnt alive on my bedroom floor.

With a grunt, I gathered my remaining strength and hauled myself up onto the windowsill, wincing as the strain brought a dizzying wave of pain that made my head spin.

My arms trembled as I tried to force myself the last few inches out the window, fear crippling my efforts.

A crash nearby had me glancing over my shoulder.

He was by the bed, throwing Bill's body at my feet.

I hesitated on the edge. Would he help me, or should I take my chance with the drop?

He didn't give me a second to think about it. Yanking me back into the room, he pressed me to his chest and scooped me up. The flames licked at my skin as he ran back through my home, the walls no longer any shade of white, but a mix of orange and yellow and black.

And red.

So much red.

The tears tumbled afresh as we burst out into the evening.

'Thank you,' I mumbled. 'I need to call the police. He killed my family.'

The masked man neither stopped nor answered me.

'Please? I need your help.'

My head spun as I tried to focus on his face, my eyes itching with the effort.

He righted his bike with one hand before sitting me over the saddle.

'No,' I said, shaking my head. 'Put me down.'

But I had no fight left to give.

He forced a helmet over my face, my hair obscuring my vision.

'Stop!'

I tried to shout, but my voice failed me, and all that emerged was a crackled whisper.

The bike roared as he took his place behind me, something tightening around my stomach and holding me to him.

I wanted to fight the wave of black that tore over me, but it drew me into the darkness.

Alone.

SIX

Phoenix

There wasn't a single part of me that didn't ache with exhaustion as I pulled up to the dock with the unconscious woman crudely fastened to me. The ride had taken hours longer than usual, between trying to avoid her falling and dragging me down with her, and my own tiredness clawing at my eyes.

I'd never been so happy to see Old Bess, my adapted fishing boat, bobbing a gentle greeting from her place on the water. It might not be the most conventional home, but it had been the only one I'd had since mine was decimated.

It was far more comfortable since I'd pushed my uncle overboard fifteen years ago.

Releasing the straps I'd used to join the woman to me, I slid her to the ground gently beside my bike and looked down at her comatose face. So pale. Was she dead? I'd be pissed if I'd carted a dead body halfway across the country.

Crouching down, I swept some of her toffee-coloured

hair from her face before removing my gloves and pressing my fingers to her throat. Despite the hole in her chest, a faint yet steady thrum met me.

Exhaling slowly, I looked her over.

Blood crusted the front of what had once been an expensive dress—all sweet and white, and a far contrast to its current state. Why had Massimo wanted her dead, though?

My eyes flicked to my boat and then back to the woman. It had been a monumental fuckup to have taken her out of the house. It was against every single one of my rules. Regret nibbled away at my stomach.

How long would it be before an investigation found that one of the four corpses was an older male rather than a woman in her twenties? Would Massimo assume she'd got away, or would he come for me? I could only hope my fire was thorough enough to have left nothing but bones in a great pile of charred debris.

Standing up, I let out a groan as my back clicked. The sooner I got her aboard, the quicker I could get out to sea and get some sleep.

I'd worry about what I'd do with her after. If she survived the next few days.

Pulling her limp form into my arms, I headed aboard, smiling as the rusted, old exterior gave way to the pristine luxury inside. It was a tight squeeze walking down the wooden stairwell to my bedroom beneath the deck. She landed on the bed without a sound, her sooty, blood-splattered arm lolling to the side.

I should have put down some towels.

Working quickly, I loaded my bike on board and stored it in the locker behind the helm.

The sun crept over the horizon as I headed out to sea, the morning light painting the waves in a wash of red and gold.

Like an ocean of flames.

Beautiful.

By noon the shore was nothing but a speck on the horizon, and I dragged my weary arse downstairs.

My new roomie was still out for the count, and still alive.

I needed to clean her wound and stitch her back up, but my eyes burned, struggling to stay open with each passing second. Trying to fix her now would almost certainly result in sloppy mistakes, and if I wanted to keep her, I'd have to be careful.

Keep her.

The very thought was dark and delicious.

Though I tried not to wallow in it, loneliness often clung to me like an angry little demon on my shoulder. Unfortunately for the woman, there was no opposing angel to fight her cause. I could keep her. No-one would know.

Even if the police had noticed she was missing, they'd never know to come for me. And Massimo knew nothing bar my bank details and my number, both of which were protected by multiple layers of security. He'd have a bugger of a time to track me down if he wanted to. Even then, I'd deny all knowledge of her.

It was perfect.

Finally, a gift from the universe just for me.

I knew it was wrong, but I didn't care enough to deny myself the pleasure that bubbled up inside of me.

The mattress dipped as I climbed onto the bed next to her and scrutinised her.

She was pretty and soft in a way that made me wish I could sink my teeth into her. The warmth of her body against mine was incredibly soothing. My arm instinctively found its place around her waist, pulling her closer to me.

She let out a little breath, and I watched eagerly, waiting to see if she'd open her eyes.

Nothing.

A smattering of freckles covered her nose, drawing my finger to them. I traced my way along her cheek before following the dried tear tracks that punctuated her sooty cheeks, marking a path down to her lips.

The impulse to press my fingers into her mouth was overwhelming.

Unhinged.

I knew I had to fight whatever urges stirred within me, but having this pretty, broken little thing in my bed was a heady temptation.

A yawn stole over me, and I rested my hand back down over her waist, the crispy red streaks of her dress rough against my fingers.

When I wake up, I thought, *I'll clean her up and fix her.*

Mend her like a broken toy that's been discarded. Stitch her up. If she survived, she'd become my most prized possession. I wouldn't be so careless with her.

My eyes fluttered shut as I teetered on the edge of sleep. I wanted to remove my lower face mask to stop the itching, however, if she woke, she might be even more frightened . So I'd hide my monstrous side—or sides—from her.

For now, at least.

Sighing, I breathed her in. She smelled like smoke and copper. As sleep finally claimed me, I smiled to myself, imagining what her soft, clean skin would smell like while she lay beside me.

SEVEN

Laura

An odd little tug at my chest made me squirm in bed, my soft sheets bunching beneath my sticky skin.

Why was I so hot?

A sharp piercing sensation jolted me out of that plane between sleeping and awake, my eyes snapping open as a curse died in my raspy throat.

A dryness filled my mouth, and my tongue lay swollen and sore against my teeth. Inhaling made my lungs burn as I stared at an unfamiliar wooden ceiling. The panelling was in a soft, smooth-looking oak that made my brain stutter.

The same strange tugging sensation had me looking down at my chest, where a set of calloused hands pressed a needle into my bare flesh. Panic ripped through me, and I tried to roll away from the dark pair of eyes focused on my face.

Rough rope secured both my wrists and ankles to the bed.

'Let me go,' I croaked as the events at my home came

crashing back into my mind. The fire. The blood. The masked man.

His lower face remained covered by a stretchy cloth mask emblazoned with that same phoenix emblem, but the heavy gas mask was gone.

He didn't answer my plea. With a forceful hand on my ribcage, he pinned me to the bed and resumed his stitching at a hole in my chest.

'Please, take me to a hospital. You need to let me go to the police. He killed my family.'

Each sharp pierce of the needle took my breath away as the man ignored me entirely, focusing only on the neat little stitches that knitted my flesh back together. When I attempted to pull away, he gave me a pointed look with those inky brown eyes and dug his fingertips harder into my ribs.

It took a few moments for the reality of my situation to hit me. My cheeks flamed at the lack of my clothing. He must have removed my dress, leaving me in nothing but a pair of panties. I tensed my fists, feeling the ropes tighten at the movement, anger flooding me to replace the shame my near nakedness brought.

It's so he can stitch you.

I hoped the little voice inside my head was right.

He's trying to help.

Idiot. Helping me would have been calling an ambulance, not stitching me like a sock that needed darning.

Closing my eyes to hide from his intense gaze, I took a slow breath. If he'd intended to kill me, he wouldn't be trying to help me.

But maybe that was worse. If he didn't want to kill me, what was his intention?

He had to be one of Massimo's associates, and Massimo tried to kill me. My family were all dead. No-one would be looking for me.

There was no saviour on the horizon. Once I thought Massimo was one, but instead he'd ripped my world to shreds.

A tear trickled down over my cheeks as the memory of my family's bodies sparked into my mind. Mum's perfect white dining room soaked in scarlet and burning to a crisp. They were far from perfect, but they'd been all I had known.

The pain in my chest continued as I willed myself not to flinch. I wouldn't give the insane masked fucker the chance to enjoy it.

Eventually, he stopped. A finger turned my face toward his, and reluctantly, I opened my eyes. He held up a washcloth and a tub of soapy water, before pressing the warm, wet cloth over my wound.

The intimacy of the touch made my stomach turn, and his dark eyes watched every movement I made as he continued to clean the blood and dirt from my skin. The tenderness almost made it worse, each stroke of the warm cloth felt good, loving, like I was precious. From someone I wanted, it would have made me feel cherished, but from the man who had kidnapped me? It disgusted me.

Turning my face from him, I let my mind go elsewhere, trying my damndest to pretend the psycho washing me didn't exist.

I had no idea how long I had been out of it, or where I was.

The room was modest but plushly decorated in rich polished woods and cream leather. My brows creased as I noted the small, circular windows, and nothing but blue outside.

The motion around us struck with such clarity that it took my breath away. We were on a boat.

My pulse thundered at the realisation my situation was even more dire than I'd thought. Not only had the man taken me, but how on earth could I hope to escape?

If I even survived his makeshift nursing.

Fuck.

Maybe death would be a kinder end.

A tap on my cheek had me turning my head slowly back to him. He was holding out a bottle of clear liquid for me.

Antiseptic.

He undid the cap and placed it above my left breast, his fingers lightly trembling at the proximity to my nipple.

His other hand moved up to slide into my fingers, grasping them. I couldn't pull away with the way I remained tied, so I had little choice but to let him hold my hand.

Then he poured.

A sob tore from my throat as the antiseptic burned like acid against my crudely stitched wound. His eyebrows furrowed when I writhed against the bed, trying to escape the blazing sensation. His fingers squeezed mine, and I returned the action, forcing my pain in through my grip and onto him.

He let me.

Placing the bottle down, he wiped the excess from my skin before disentangling his fingers from mine.

'Who are you?' I asked, my voice weak.

Rising to his feet, he just looked at me before shaking his head.

'Please, just a name?'

Nothing.

He covered me with a soft blanket before heading out of the room, leaving me to sob on the gently bobbing bed.

I should have been getting married.

Instead, a masked man had tied me to his bed, on a boat, probably in the middle of the sea. My family was dead. My life, gone.

Death would be a blessing.

EIGHT

Laura

Bright light hitting my face pulled me from the depths of sleep. Confusion swarmed my mind as I tried to roll over, a deep ache tugging at my chest. Tightness held my wrists fast, something rough biting into my skin as I attempted to move.

With a groan, I forced my eyes open.

The gravity of my predicament hit me with a punch. Ropes bound my wrists, and through the small, round window, I could see the sun sinking low beyond the endless blue horizon. Not to mention how exposed I felt from the lack of clothing underneath the thin blanket covering me.

And then, there was him.

He sat silently on a chair by the bed, stalking me with his stare.

Eyes as dark as sin. That dreadful mask covering half of his face. Swallowing hard through the dry scrape of my parched throat, I contemplated my options.

Which were incredibly few.

Did I accept my fate and take whatever he intended on inflicting on me? Did I fight? Kill him and try to find my way to land? Did I play pretend until I could convince him to take me back to shore?

Rationally, the last option was the only viable one.

I had to make him trust me enough to bring me back to civilisation.

He shifted in the seat, leaning forward so his elbows rested on his thighs, his head tilting just a touch while his eyes roved over me.

Pin pricks crept across my stomach at his open stare, panic flooding my system. How could I play pretend in the face of a predator?

He leant forward, and I flinched, the rope digging further into my skin.

'Please,' I whispered, my words catching in my throat. 'Please, untie me.'

Those dark eyes narrowed, moving from my face to my red, chafed wrists. My stomach knotted as he stood, towering over the bed, his head nearly scuffing the roof of the low cabin ceiling. Reaching behind him, he picked up a marker pen from a thin desk and began to write on the mirror.

The black ink pen squeaked against the reflective surface, making me wince as I watched words take form in large, black letters.

NO SCREAMING
NO RUNNING
NO FIGHTING

I nodded my head when his eyes met mine in the reflection. It wasn't a promise if I didn't say it aloud.

Within three steps he was by my side, I shifted slightly to make a little more space between us, the thin blanket falling away from my chest. His nostrils flared, and his gaze dropped to my exposed breasts. Lifting his hand, he grazed two fingers along my collarbone, making me want to sob. Swallowing hard, I forced the emotions down. I just had to hold it together long enough for him to untie me and get to a weapon.

I could do that.

I had to.

I expected him to squeeze my breasts, or graze my nipples, but he didn't. With a gentleness that turned my stomach, he traced the edge of the stitching he'd performed the previous night.

With a seemingly satisfying nod, he withdrew his hand and thrust it into the pocket of his dark camo trousers. The knife he brought out glittered in the morning sun, the blade bursting out as he pressed a button. It took every ounce of my willpower not to cry out.

Just act good.

Just a little longer.

Placing one knee on the bed beside me, he slid the blade along the soft skin of my inner forearm. The scratch of it made my nipples peak and shame filled me.

What the fuck was that?

Putting my body's reaction down to stress, I held my breath until he slid the sharp metal through the ropes like they were butter. Fighting down the flight response, I took his hand as he pulled me into a sitting position.

My fingers trembled when he took my wrists into his hands, rubbing feeling back into them. Every part of me screamed to attack him. To fight the gentle touches like a cornered animal. To slash and punch and kick.

While his attention focused on my wrists, I took a moment to truly look at my captor.

The mask covering his lower face was weathered, the phoenix on it faded with age. Old scars webbed the left side of his face, extending from his cheekbones, all the way up to his hairline. Pitted and taught, they marked the skin like a series of mountains on a map. A tiny flicker of pity lit in my chest, but I quickly extinguished it.

No matter his past, he had no right to take me prisoner. Feeling sorry for an injured lion made it no less likely to hurt you. I stifled a moan as his fingers worked my aching wrists and palms, inviting the blood to flow right back into my fingers. The touch of a monster shouldn't make me swoon. I pulled my fingers, and his grip tightened. My pulse picked up in my throat as he continued to stare at my wrist.

'I need to use the bathroom,' I said after a few moments of strained silence.

Dropping my massaged wrists into my lap, he got up and left the bedroom without another look.

I swiftly let myself into the minuscule bathroom that joined the bedroom cabin to relieve myself.

Desperate to find anything that might be useful, my eyes wandered the tiny room.

Shampoo. Shower gel. Toothpaste.

Fuck.

Eventually, my gaze fell on the glass shower door, and I wondered if I could use a piece of it as a makeshift knife.

Unfortunately, I'd probably just cut myself rather than injure the weirdo.

I scrubbed my hands over my face and let out a muffled, frustrated groan.

After flushing the toilet, I washed my hands, scrubbing the soap into my skin so vigorously that the rope burns stung anew.

I couldn't just sit on the motherfucking boat and be his toy.

I needed to get back to England. To get to the authorities and have them put Massimo and my captor behind bars for their sins. For what they'd done to me and my family.

A little voice in my head taunted me. *They deserved it.*

Screwing my eyes shut, I shook the deranged thought from my mind.

The little mirror above the sink barely showed my whole face when I opened my eyes. Standing on my toes, I examined the wound on my chest. It ached something fearsome whenever I lifted my arm, and the skin around the crude black stitches was purpling up toward my neck.

You could be dead.

You should have been dead.

The man I thought was my freedom pushed me into this floating cage, and I fully intended to kill him.

Right after taking out the asshole aboard.

Pulling on a hoodie and pair of shorts from the bedroom, I walked through the innards of the boat, stopping at a galley kitchen. Glancing toward the door that led out onto the deck, I saw no sign of the masked man. My pulse skipped as I opened one of the drawers, hunting through the utensils in search of potential weapons.

Unless I could mash his brains with a potato masher, there was nothing useful.

Bar a rolling pin, nada in the next drawer down.

Frustration made me growl as I slammed door after cupboard door. Wrenching open the last one, I saw a block of knives. With sweat gathering at the base of my spine, I glanced back at the doorway. The wooden handle was rough in my palm as I clenched my fingers so tightly that they began to whiten.

Even with a weapon, how did I think it would go down?

You're an idiot, Laura.

Probably a soon-to-be-dead idiot.

But that was better than nothing.

The deck of the boat was neat but worn, a far cry from the plush-looking interior. Rust clung to any metallic, dulling its shine. The rough flooring scratched at my bare feet when I inched quietly toward the silhouetted figure that stood at the bow, looking out over the sea.

The vast fucking sea.

If I couldn't stab him, maybe I could just shunt him overboard.

Squeezing the blade of the kitchen knife, I tried to amp myself up for what I needed to do. The closer I crept, the more his massive stature sent concern through me. His back was packed with muscle beneath the thin t-shirt he wore, and his biceps were like fucking tree trunks.

My mouth dried out with every step toward the beast of a man. The silent creep.

My heart beat so fast I worried he'd be able to hear it. It would give me away before I could strike.

My palm slickened around the knife, making it more

difficult to grip. I desperately wanted to shift the blade to my other hand and wipe my sweaty palm on my clothing, but I didn't dare make any movement I didn't need to.

So close.

Holding my breath, I lifted the blade and lunged forward, striking it down toward the left side of his upper back. He turned right as I made my move and caught the slash on his upper arm—more of a graze that drew a dark red line, really. His hand fit over my wrist, squeezing as I panted. Pain filled my arm, but I held onto the knife, determined not to let him win.

Amusement danced in his eyes, and I wanted nothing more than to see him dead.

Grabbing the blade with my other hand, I sliced wildly at him while kicking and pushing against him in an attempt to launch him over the railing.

He reacted like my attack was that of a child—like it was nothing.

I let out an angry scream and shoved hard. He let go of my wrist at the same time and slid out of my way.

My foot slipped, and I toppled toward the waist-high rail.

'No,' I gasped, dropping the knife and hearing it clatter on the deck. Time slowed. My balance tipped as I hit the rail, sending me right over the edge.

For a few long moments, only air wrapped itself around me.

Then, I hit the water in a wall of cold that stole my breath right from my chest.

Fighting the shock, I kicked my legs and fought to find the surface amid the panic rising inside me. Nothing but icy water around me, and nothing to hold on to either.

With a great heaving sob, I broke the surface, turning myself to look for the boat.

'Help me,' I panted to the lone figure leaning against the railing, watching me suffer.

Silence.

'Please.' Cold numbed my extremities, making treading the water all the more difficult. 'I'm sorry.'

Nothing.

'I'm scared. I've lost everyone, and I want to go home.' Hot tears mingled with the frigid saltwater that streaked my face.

Beneath the surface, something nudged at my thigh. Fear enveloped me as I tried to look around me. Something rough grazed my calf, and I let out a scream.

I wasn't as alone as I thought.

NINE

Phoenix

Water slapped against her chest, its noise drowned out by the absolute ruckus she was making.

I could see a large shape surrounding her flailing form beneath the water. The shark must have been curious about what was causing all the splashing.

Thankfully, the only sharks that tended to frequent the area were basking sharks. They don't even have teeth.

I hadn't wanted to laugh quite so much in a very long time.

Even soaked to the head, she still had that spark in her eyes—like an ember plucked straight from the fire.

My pretty little ember.

'Please, help me?' she called, her voice even more panicked than before.

My arm still bled from the cut she'd inflicted on me—not too deep, at least. Thin rivulets of blood snaked down over my forearm, wrapping my fingers like scarlet gloves.

I had a choice. I could leave her there to tire and sink. The sea would rid me of the issue of dealing with my first mistake in years.

Or I could use her misfortune to my advantage.

To make her behave.

Leaning over the bobbing helm of the boat, I held my hand out and tensed my bicep. A fresh slew of blood dripped from the cut and followed its crimson path to my fingers, which I stretched out over the water.

'What are you doing?' Her words hit me, and I looked down at her stricken face. A slop of salt water hit her right in the face, making her cough.

A drop of my blood fell into the ocean. This wasn't the first blood I'd lost to it while out on my uncle's goddamned boat.

No, he'd seen to me losing plenty over the years.

'Stop it. Are you... insane...' she shouted. Her squeals as the basking shark slipped past her made my cock twitch. I wanted to make her squeal like that.

'Please.' Fear filled her big doe eyes. They darted from left to right as she tried to paddle back toward the boat, which was drifting slowly away from her. 'I'll do anything. I'm sorry! Okay?'

Lifting an eyebrow, I backed away from the edge and toward the cabin. Her wild screams and curses followed me. A chuckle sounded deep in my throat, silenced only when it reached my mouth. The feeling of the noise made me stop in my tracks.

Touching a hand to my throat, I made it again. The vibrations pulsed down my fingers. It felt... good. So fucking good.

If only it could come out fully.

I grabbed a chunky permanent marker from the kitchen and walked back to my screaming flame.

'You absolute arsehole. Get me out of this water.'

I shook my head and dropped to my stomach, leaning over the edge beneath the railings.

The pen squeaked against the boat's finish, black streaks forming upside-down letters.

ANYTHING?

'What?' she called.

I underlined the word. Twice.

Her eyebrows creased until eventually she figured it out.

'Yes, I'll do anything if you get me out of here. Anything!'

I reached down and wrote one more word below my first.

PROMISE?

Not that I thought I could particularly trust the word of the woman who tried to stab me and shove me off my own boat. Hopefully, she'd stick to her word this time.

If not I'd have to get creative with punishments.

'Yes. I promise.' She let out a blood-curdling scream before bursting into tears. 'I'll do anything you say. Cook for you. Clean up. Scrub the deck. I'll be good. I can please you. I can even suck your fucking cock. Just get me back aboard.'

Scrub the deck. Fuck, I wanted to laugh again.

Fucking precious.

I threw down one of the life preserver rings attached to a rope and watched as she clung desperately to it.

The basking shark had long lost interest, but she couldn't see that from her point of view.

She slipped the ring around her body and gripped the rope. Pulling deadweight—soggy deadweight—on my own was harder than I'd imagined. My forearms throbbed, veins bulging like giant bevelled cracks. Sweat beaded on my brows as I yanked, my boots barely holding their grip on the deck.

At last, the top of her head appeared, and I tied off the rope before going to her. Reaching over the rail, I slid one hand into the back of her hair, fisting it tight.

'I promise,' she repeated through chattering teeth as she stared up at me.

Blue tinged her full lips, and I craved nothing more than warming them back up with my own.

The thought came with a heat that soon turned to ash against my tongue. That wasn't for me.

Taking the rope in my other hand, I hauled her aboard, dumping her unceremoniously onto the deck.

'Thank you,' she whimpered, unhooking the ring and pulling herself up on unsteady feet.

A violent shiver stole over her body. She needed to lose the wet clothes.

She all but growled when I pushed the top up over her head, leaving her bare-chested. The breeze whipped past us, sending her skin pebbling in its wake.

I bent to my knees, removing the rest of her clothes with firm tugs. The sopping clothes clung to her, almost as if resistant to let her go.

'Couldn't wait until I was dry? Well, get it over with,' she said. I stilled at the glare she fixed me with. As much as I wanted to hear her squeal, fucking a half-frozen woman wasn't my jam. No, there was time for that later. I wanted her screams of pleasure, and she would beg for my cock before I'd let her have it.

Standing up, I reached forward, ignoring her flinch, and took her by the elbow.

Her eyes lit with a combative glare, but it quickly extinguished as she leaned heavily into my grip.

Between her bullet wound and the cold water, her strength had left her entirely.

Moving behind her, I tried to scoop her into my arms, yet she shrugged me off with a snarl.

'I'll walk,' she muttered. And step by shaky step, never allowing more than the briefest support from my hand, she did.

TEN

Laura

I hated him.

I hated that I needed his steady hand to get me back to the cabin, tremors shaking my frozen limbs. I'd failed. Spectacularly.

Instead of securing my freedom, I'd offered him even more of myself to get him to rescue me for a second time.

Cold cut deep into my bones by the time we'd made it down into the bedroom.

Wrapping my arms over my chest, I sat unsteadily on the end of the bed. I shrunk away as he walked past me. What was I going to do? I had to behave until I could get to somewhere I could have an actual chance at escape. But how? How could I let him take whatever he wanted and survive it?

Another shiver stole through me as he rummaged in a closet, pulling out a large hoodie and a pair of black jogging bottoms. He handed them to me with barely a glance and left the room.

The hoodie was old and worn, its soft, thick fabric hugging me when I pulled it over my shoulders. A touch of comfort amongst the god-forbidden boat that had become an oversized prison cell. The pants were snug around my hips, but I was glad to be covered from neck to ankle, considering the promise I'd made to do whatever he wanted me to.

Crushing myself into a compact armchair to the left of the bed, I crossed my arms over one another, wrapping them around my knees.

Those intense eyes settled on me, sending a tremor along my spine. His boots squeaked against the floor as he rounded the bed, heading straight for me. Every muscle in my body seized on his approach.

He thrust a mug into my hands, heat radiating into my icy fingers. Milky brown tea sloshed gently as the boat bobbed, and the familiar sensation of comfort filled me. Tears pricked my eyes as I stared down at the hot tea, avoiding the man sitting across from me on the bed, his knees grazing the edge of my chair.

Silence enveloped the room, only punctuated by my occasional sips of the sweetened tea. My stomach grumbled as I drank, reminding me just how long it had been since I'd last eaten.

He heard it too, his gaze dipping to my middle, his brows creasing.

'What's your name?' I asked, needing some sort of noise to break the quiet.

Nothing. I sighed, placing my now empty mug on the dresser by the bed and wrapping my arms back around my knees.

'My name's Laura. I don't know if you know who I am, or how much Massimo told you.'

His fingers twitched against the bed cover, but he remained silent.

'I don't have a home. I don't have anyone waiting for me. I've got nothing.' The blue water undulated outside the window beside me as I spoke, and I focused on the distant spot where the sea met the sky. 'You can use me. I agreed to that. But you can't make me be anything other than a human fleshlight for you. I'll hate every minute of it, and I will get away from you the first chance I get.'

Swallowing hard, I continued to watch that spot far from me and my predicament.

Then his fingers gripped my hand.

The urge to snatch them away flared in me, but instead, I narrowed my eyes at him and held firm. I wouldn't break. That's probably what he wanted, to see me begging for him to leave me alone. I wouldn't give him the satisfaction. I'd be a sack of potatoes; unresponsive and dull. He'd get bored and leave me be. Hell, maybe he'd get so bored he'd drop me at the next port.

A movement against my palm directed my eyes toward it. His fingers were scarred on the left hand which held mine in place. Red and white webbing decorated the digits and spread up his wrist. With his unscarred right pointer finger, he drew a shape into my palm.

Confusion filled me at the ticklish touch. What was he doing?

A line, and a semi-circle. A P?

He was spelling something.

PH...

The caress of his fingers sent a warmth through me that made me want to retch. The tingle of a man's touch had been something I'd dreamt about in the lead up to my wedding. My non-wedding. Yet, here were the tingles, with a psycho.

OE

I chewed on my bottom lip as he continued.

NIX

After he drew the last letter, his gaze flicked up to my face and lingered on my bottom lip, which was caught between my teeth. He closed his eyes for a moment as he took a shaky breath.

'Phoenix?' I asked, putting the letters together.

He nodded.

It made sense of the worn embroidered bird on his masks.

My stomach growled viciously, sending roiling discomfort through me.

He stood, hesitating for a moment before stroking a finger across my bottom lip, right where my teeth had been. Blood still stained his arm from where I'd cut him, and it took every piece of willpower I had not to lash out at his touch.

He left me there with my empty mug, and the whisper of his touch tainting my lips.

ELEVEN

Phoenix

The blender churned, filling the kitchenette with the scent of strawberry. The powder and milk slowly combined until they turned that familiar smooth shade of pink. Only that day, I'd made a double helping. The high-calorie shake was as much a part of my routine as breathing. I never had to worry about what to cook or what I fancied,; it was always the same. Milk. Powder. Blend.

Pouring half of the mixture into a glass, I grabbed a straw and pushed it down into the thick liquid. Checking over my shoulder, I slid my mask down over my chin and pushed the straw through the tiny gap on the left side of what should have been my mouth.

A burst of sweet strawberry flavour washed over my tongue as I drank the shake down. Bar a child-sized toothbrush and toothpaste, it was the only thing I ever forced through the small opening. Even the toothbrush head took some force. The doctors had told my uncle that oral health was important, and I never forgot it. Even if we'd never gone back to have the surgeries that would have opened my burned, fused lips, I'd still always secretly hoped the day would come.

As months turned to years, and the scars solidified, I saw that dream die and embraced what I was. A monster living beneath the surface, someone people called upon but never wanted beyond their nefarious purposes. I was just another tool.

A noise behind me startled me, and I pulled the straw from my mouth before yanking my mask back into place.

Laura stood sheepishly in the doorway, her still wet hair brushed through and the empty tea mug loose in her hand.

I eyed it, half expecting her to throw it at my head.

I filled a second glass with the high-calorie sludge, offering it to her. With reluctance, she set down the empty mug and sat at the low table, casting a sceptical glance at the drink.

When she failed to take a sip, I grabbed the packet of powder and laid it on the table before her.

She had two choices; eat or starve.

'Is this all you have?' she said, scanning the packet with a frown.

I nodded.

She took a little sip and swallowed, a grimace crossing her pretty face. The drink might not be tasty, but it would stop the grumbling coming from her stomach. No wonder she'd been acting like a caged animal. The first rule of taming a pet was making sure it didn't go hungry. I'd need to keep her belly full before I started filling her everywhere else.

Excitement threaded through me as I watched her lick a drop of strawberry shake from her lower lip, imagining it was my cum she lapped up so delicately.

Even in my hoodie and jogging bottoms, Laura looked delicious. The way her cheeks rounded so softly. The way my hoodie stretched around her chest. Seeing her walking through my boat naked had been the most divine torture. The temptation to bend her over and warm her with my hips crashing into her ass while she shivered from the cold had made me ache with desperation.

Soon.

Patience.

I doubted I'd be able to hold her captive forever without her stabbing me in the throat at some point, but damn would I make the most of the time I could keep her.

The stacks of money I'd amassed in my illicit work meant a quick fuck was always easy to find. Money meant nothing was out of reach. But I wanted more. I wanted to feel Laura fall apart under my fingers. I wanted to make her crave my touch even though she hated me. To make her beg for my cock even as she cringed at the scars that marred my face.

I needed to feel wanted, even if it was only until the post-orgasm shame swept over her.

I winced as I stacked the dishes into the compact dishwasher. The cut on my arm wasn't deep, but it stung like a bitch.

While Laura sipped her drink and forced it down like a good girl, I retrieved the first aid kit from one of the cabinets and set about cleaning up the wound.

The little fucker smiled when I shuddered at the sharp sting of the antiseptic, those big doe eyes watching my suffering with glee.

Pain and I were old friends. I'd been through so much worse.

I finished with my arm as she swallowed the last of the milky liquid and sat back on the bench.

'So what now?' she asked, her words hesitant.

A visit to the cottage was on the cards, but I neither could nor I cared to tell her that. Instead, I closed the distance between us, enjoying the widening of her eyes with each step.

Her lower lip quivered as I ran my finger gently over her jawline, fear sparking across her lovely features. Sinking my fingers deep into her wet hair, I tipped her head back and drew my face close to hers, inhaling deeply.

In all the years it had been melted shut, never had I wanted to be able to open my stupid fucking mouth and taste something so desperately.

Fuck, I wanted to devour her.

She let out a little squeak that had my dick straining against my pants.

Her fear was enough to stoke me—for now.

I simply shrugged as she took a shaky breath, and my cheek twitched, the closest to a smile I'd had in an eon.

When I walked out onto the deck, glass smashed against the door, an angry screech following the crash.

That's it, Laura. Feed the rage. It'll stoke my fire, my little ember.

TWELVE

Laura

The boat moved steadily as the day turned from bright to an orange blaze, eventually dipping into darkness.

Boredom ate at me in the silence of the bedroom. Phoenix hadn't come to see me other than to hand me another god-awful shake. The highly sweetened creamy liquid tasted awful. He didn't seem to be forthcoming with any actual food, however, so I drank it through gritted teeth.

Moonlight reflected across the waves, like great glittering, never-ending scales on some behemoth of a beast. Where were we going? The boat seemed to move with purpose, heading in one direction.

With a sigh, I opted to go out and ask him. It had to be better than sitting there and wondering.

Opening the bedroom door, a hauntingly beautiful series of notes wrapped their way around me. Muffled at first, they became clearer with each step I took toward the deck. Creeping along the wall of the wheelhouse, I headed toward the sweet, yet morose music as if pulled toward it by some sort of magic.

Phoenix stood near the bow of the boat, a violin resting just below his chin, his fingers artfully pulling a melody from its fraught strings. His hands moved swiftly, caressing the bow across the bridge and making the old violin sing as prettily as any sea siren. I stilled, watching him.

Two large metal bins burned between us, throwing a bright orange glow over his muscled forearms which danced under the ministrations of his playing. Tendons stood out amongst the veined muscles on one arm, while the other was webbed with the same scarring which marked his face and neck. His eyes were closed, the warm light dancing across his features, lost utterly in the rapturous music.

It was a beautiful sight. I wanted to revel in it almost as much as I wanted to tear it apart. He was supposed to be a monster.

Even the devil loves music.

A sad smile twitched at my lip. My mother had often said it, trying to tell me that giving into temptations would lead to trouble. But being the good girl had landed me here. Stuck on a boat with a man who I'd agreed to let use me for whatever he wanted, miles from home and completely alone.

I'd played her game. Agreed to marry for the family cause. What did it get me? A hole in the chest and a swim with fucking sharks.

I was done playing by anyone else's rules.

Getting Phoenix to believe I was the submissive, weak woman was my goal. Then I'd kill him. Drive a knife through his neck until he choked on his own blood.

My breath caught when I caught his gaze locked onto me, his eyebrows dipping as though he could read my thoughts.

He tipped his head toward a low bench beside one of the fiery bins, and I reluctantly made my way to it.

Firelight warmed my face, his fingers not letting up on the violin, pulling ever sweeter notes from her while I focused on the dark horizon far in the distance. I closed my eyes and let the music wash over me, letting myself pretend I was at one of Mother's parties, surrounded by people who knew me.

The bobbing of the boat along with the music lulled me into a place of peace, and I let my muscles relax. Exhaustion tingled through my body. Between the healing bullet wound in my chest and my dip in the sea, I was desperately tired.

A hand caressed through my hair, and I moaned softly before jolting away from the touch.

I hadn't even noticed the music ending.

Phoenix sat next to me, the violin resting on the bench.

Be meek. I told myself. *Trick him.*

My breath hitched. He ran his scarred fingers along my collar bone, stopping at my pulse point and closing his eyes. Fear made my heart beat faster, and his fingers pressed more firmly into the hollow of my neck. Tracing his other hand against my thigh he spelled out a word.

SCARED?

I nodded, keeping my focus on his dark eyes, the fire's reflection dancing in them.

Was he going to fuck me?

To my dismay the bile the thought brought was swiftly followed by a pulsating between my thighs. It had been a long time since I'd let myself fall into bed with someone. I'd been waiting for Massimo. Our love story was going to be one for the ages. I'd been so sure of it.

Phoenix's thumb tilted my jaw up, and had it not been for the mask covering his mouth, I'd have thought he was going to kiss me. It would be one thing to endure his dick, but the softness would be too much to bear.

'Make it quick,' I begged, my words coming out strangled.

His fingers moved against my leg once more, this time on my inner thigh.

NEVER

'Please, just get it over with or let me go.' I should have stayed in the bedroom.

His throat moved as he swallowed, the phoenix emblazoned mask just millimetres from my lips. The fingers on my throat wrapped around my neck, tightening. The gasp it drew from me, made him give a deep, low groan.

GOING TO MAKE YOU BEG FOR IT

Each swipe of his finger made me hate him more.

I pushed him hard, and he relaxed back against the boat's railing as I stood, my cheeks blazing.

'I will never beg.' I spat the words at him, my promise to be meek fleeing. 'Stop toying with me. It's worse than just fucking me.'

My head spun as I backed away from him, half expecting him to chase after me. Phoenix looked completely unbothered by my reaction, sitting there as if nothing had happened.

Moving as quickly as my feet would carry me, I fled back to the cabin, shutting myself in the bedroom and pushing a chair up under the door handle. Throwing myself onto the bed, I screamed into the covers, letting all the anger and frustration pour out of me. Tears wet the pillow, and I didn't stop until my voice grew hoarse and my body grew limp.

At last, sleep took me.

Light streamed in through the windows when I awoke. Peeling my hair from my face, I groaned.

God, how long had I slept?

Rubbing at my face, I pulled myself upright, seeing the chair still wedged beneath the door and feeling a sense of satisfaction. At least I could sleep soundly knowing I could shut him out.

In the washroom, I relieved myself, hunting through the cabinet for mouthwash. My mouth tasted like I'd licked the deck clean before heading to bed.

Standing in front of the small mirror, I pulled my hoodie up, looking at the angry red scar on my chest. It was beginning to knit together, the scabs starting to fall away. Even if I made it off the boat and away from Phoenix, I'd always carry the marks of that night with me.

I'd just had to make sure the scars I left behind were much worse than the ones I carried.

Flopping back down on the bed, I looked out of the window, my heart all but stopping at the sight of a tiny harbour.

Crushing myself to the window, I saw people. Fishermen!

I banged on the window, but they were too far away to hear me.

With adrenaline pumping through my veins, I pulled the chair out from under the door handle, ready to run to the deck and throw myself overboard.

The handle wouldn't push down.

No.

Fuck, no!

Using all my strength, I rattled and hauled at the handle, desperation bubbling up inside of me and coming out in a whimper.

The door wouldn't budge.

My fists ached as I crashed them against the circular windows, my throat aching as I shouted at the far off people outside.

'Help me! Someone please help me!'

None of the fishermen so much as glanced my way.

'He's taken me. Please?!'

I picked up the chair and thrust the leg into the window, trying with every ounce of determination I could fathom to smash it. My arms ached as a jarring sensation rattled through them with each strike. The glass was too thick.

Grabbing one of the markers in the desk, I wrote on the window pane, making sure the words were back to front.

HELP ME!

An old man walked into view, along the harbour side, with his Jack Russell trailing alongside him. I banged hard on the glass. His head turned, trying to find the source of the noise.

'I'm in here! Help me!' I cried, the sides of my fists aching as I thumped as hard as I could.

Yes! It was working. He turned his head toward the boat, his eyes scanning for the thumping sound.

See me, I begged the universe, jerking my arms back and forth, trying to make as big movements as possible to attract his attention.

He'd have a phone. He'd be able to call the police. They'd come for me.

The boat shuddered, sending me toppling onto the bed. Engines kicked in, and we moved away from the harbourside.

'No,' I screamed, pulling myself back up to the window. 'Let me go you piece of shit!'

I crashed the chair into the low ceiling, rage coursing through me as the old man shook his head and continued on his walk, none the wiser that he could have saved me.

The port grew smaller and smaller in the window until it was nothing but a dashed hope in the distance.

Curling myself up into a ball in the corner of the bed, I pressed my head into my knees.

Next time, I'll be ready.

THIRTEEN

Phoenix

The island came into sight and warmth flowed through me. It was the closest thing I had to a home. I'd never taken another living being there, bar the sheep and wild ponies who roamed the tiny island, and nerves fluttered in my stomach at the thought of Laura on my land.

It had been one of the few splurges I'd allowed myself since going into the lucrative field of burning evidence for a living. My secret refuge. My terra firma.

I hoped she would love it as much as I did.

Sharp grey cliffs gave way to a sandy beach, the cove leading onto the natural harbour where I would moor the boat. Rocks jutted from the still sea, but I knew the path through them like the back of my hand. Navigating through them, I began to hum, pleasure seeping through me.

Home at last.

The island mostly consisted of rough, grassy terrain and rocky outcrops, but the pale sandy beach was my own private paradise. Sure, the weather wasn't exactly tropical being that it was in the Outer Hebrides, but the sunsets were second to none.

Would my little ember be watching our approach? Wondering where I'd taken her? My wildling, so full of rage. I'd laughed to myself at the clattering of what I assumed was the chair against the ceiling. She had fire in her veins.

Just like me.

Would she be pacified with the gifts I'd stopped to buy for her? I didn't expect a thank you, but I hoped they'd bring her a touch of joy amongst her sorrow.

My pet needed to be pleased.

So very badly.

Her whole being hummed with need. She didn't know it, but it rolled off of her in waves. I doubted I could tame such a firecracker, but I could handle it with care, stoke her flames rather than putting them out. Make her burn with me. Not against me.

The boat came into the shallow harbour, and I leapt over board, hauling the rope with me, fastening it with a habit built from so many times mooring there.

Feeling eyes on me, I glanced at the bedroom window. Angry eyes glared back at me through the words HELP ME, written in black ink.

Oh Laura, you'll be licking that off before we disembark.

The door was still firmly locked from our little trip to port, and I turned the heavy key until the lock clicked with a satisfying thunk.

Opening the door slowly, I awaited her launching herself at me. Instead, one of my boots came crashing into the wall right beside my head.

Ducking out of the way, I half grinned beneath my mask, in my own twisted manner.

My little spark was all alight.

How delightful.

I tore into the room and set myself upon her where she cowered by the bathroom, lashing out like a little hell-cat. With our size difference, there was little she could do to fight me off. Panting through my nose, I held her turned toward the window, her hair gripped firmly in my fist. Her round arse pressed against my crotch in the most maddening way and a wave of pure, unadulterated *need* washed through me. A possession of desire wrapped about me, and I pressed my nose into her hair, breathing her in as if her scent could satisfy me. It didn't. It just added fuel to the burning ache in my groin.

Fuck. Never had compulsion so strongly gripped me.

Pinning her between my hips and the wall, I grabbed the marker pen from the dresser and wrote over her words on the glass.

DIRTY GIRLS DO DIRTY THINGS.

Forcing her head back, I pinched her nose until in exasperation she opened her mouth.

'Stop it,' she whimpered, 'I'm sorry.'

Never had I wanted to speak as badly as I did around her. I had so fucking much to say. Using one finger, I wrote on the tender skin at the side of her neck.

LICK IT CLEAN

'I don't want to,' she whispered.

NOW

I thrust two fingers deep into her mouth, rubbing them over her tongue. The wet heat had my knees practically buckling. If she didn't do as I demanded, I'd soon find a much more interesting way to use her tongue.

Laura gagged when I pressed my fingers more firmly back toward her throat, fucking her mouth with them.

'Okay,' she spluttered against my fingers, spit dripping down over them.

With a tentative movement, she pressed her tongue against the glass, leaving a trail of spit.

I watched from over her shoulder, delighting in the way the arch of her back rubbed her ass against my hard dick. Paying for sex had always been easy, but the women preferred not to look at my scarred face, and I preferred to just get the deed over and done with as quickly as possible. But this? This was a whole new heady rush. Fuck, every touch drove me to a madness that I craved. When she eventually gave into me, or drove me to the point I could hold back no longer, it would be mind blowing.

Black pen gathered on her tongue as she swept it over the glass, the word dirty transferring from the pane into her mouth.

She'd never looked so fucking hot.

Yes, I wanted to croon in her ear, *that's my pretty pet.*

I shifted my grip closer to her scalp, using my hand to

direct her tongue. The HELP ME wouldn't budge after being there for hours, but my words slowly disappeared.

Much to my surprise, as I gripped harder, she let out a little moan. The sweetest sound I'd ever heard.

Redness filled her cheeks, and she tried to move away from the window. I grunted as I pressed her face back to it, making her resume her slow licking.

GOOD GIRL

I spelled out against her throat with my other hand.

A tear escaped her eye and made its way down her cheek. I traced its path with my gaze, jealous of its nearness to her. Being part of her. I wanted that.

I'd have done anything in the whole fucking world to pull my mask down and taste it.

FOURTEEN

Laura

The area we'd docked at looked utterly deserted. The sea caressed at a pale sandy beach, intermittent dark rocks jutting out from the water along the shore line. A tiny stone cottage sat alone a little ways back from the beach, surrounded by nothing but trees, rugged grassy terrain and some distant cliffs.

Where were we?

If I'd have arrived here with anyone other than my captor, I might have described it as a perfect little slice of paradise. A pretty hideaway.

Instead, it was like a green cage. A bigger cage than the boat, sure. But no less isolated.

I only hoped that beyond the trees there were other people. A village when I could find help. A phone. Something. *Anything.*

Phoenix jumped over the gap between the boat and the wooden jetty, before reaching out for my hand. I ignored it and made the jump myself, my stomach in my chest as I looked down at the narrow gap. Still, getting squished between the boat and the dock would be better than willingly taking his hand. I landed on two feet before stumbling a step forward.

He carried numerous bags, picking his way over the stony ground that led to the patch beyond the beach. I followed, my legs feeling like they were at least half noodle after days on the constantly moving boat.

The ground was outrageously solid in comparison.

A hare darted across the path, disappearing into the long, untamed grass. Pebbles on the path dug into my bare feet with every step. What had happened to my shoes after Phoenix had taken me from the fire?

No idea.

Stepping onto the grass at the side of the path, I looked back at the spot where the hare had vanished. Phoenix trudged along the path toward the cottage, not looking back at all.

My heart thumped in my chest.

I dashed into the grass, following the hare.

Adrenaline fuelled my run until I hit a patch of trees, not looking back to see if Phoenix gave chase. My breaths became laboured as my thighs burned, the stitches in my chest tightening with every harried step.

Eventually, my legs could carry me no further, and I collapsed in a pile against a tree trunk, trying to breath through the ache in my lungs. I'd run uphill, through the trees, only stopping when they opened up to a new view.

A view that made my heart sink.

It was an island. A tiny fucking island. The cottage was

the sole property on it. From the high point I could see the sea on all sides, wild sheep scattered through the open ground, grazing on the long grass.

Hot tears filled my eyes and I lashed out at the tree, catching my knuckles on the rough bark. Frustration fuelled my strikes and I didn't let up until my knuckles were bloody. Stumbling along the ridge, I found myself standing on one of the low cliffs, looking out over the never ending sea.

No-one was going to come for me.

Phoenix must have let me run, knowing there was nowhere to go.

My feet carried me to the edge of the grass topped cliff. Dizziness swept through me at the sight of the sea crashing into the rocks far below.

Just jump.

It could all be over so quickly. I was supposed to die in the fire, and what was the point of continuing? To be Phoenix's toy? Then what? Wait until he grows bored of me and hope for release? Yeah, right. He'd be more likely to bury me on this remote island where no-one would ever find me.

What if he left me there? Alone.

The tears came heavy, cascading down my cheeks until my hoodie grew sodden around my neck. I took another step closer to the edge, my toes no longer on the solid ground. Fear strangled my sobs and I closed my eyes, ready.

It would be quick.

I hoped.

Peace filled me, and I let a tiny smile cross my lips.

A snicker pulled me from my reverie, making me look down as panic swept up and filled me. I stumbled backward.

Fuck.

I'd almost done it.

I collapsed against the grass, throwing myself downward and letting the sobs take over. Curling into a foetal position, I let all of the pent up anguish escape. Tears gave way to sobs, and sobs gave way to desperate cries that sounded alien even to myself.

Death keeps coming so close, but I keep narrowly missing it. It has to be better than staying with Phoenix.

I jolted as something soft and warm nudged my neck. I'd been so lost in my near jump, I hadn't noticed another creature sharing the space with me.

A short pony stood above me, the heat from its nostrils blowing through my hair as it curiously sniffed me.

A surprised laugh erupted from my mouth, and a delirium filled me. The pony didn't seem to mind, it moved down to sniff along my neckline.

Pulling myself to sit, I reached out and stroked the velvety soft skin of its nose.

'Well, hi,' I crooned, sniffling down snot and tears. The pony let me take what I needed, as if it was some magical beast sent by the universe itself in a moment where I needed someone kind more than anything else.

'I don't suppose you have a phone?' I said through a tortured chuckle. The pony thrust its head against my chest, nudging me. I gave it a rub along the jaw and sighed. 'Guess not. But this'll do.'

Wind swept up over the cliff face, whipping my hair around us.

'At least I'm not the only one stuck here,' I whispered, pressing my face into the soft fur of the pony's neck.

We could be companions in our desolation.

FIFTEEN

Phoenix

Footsteps crunching in the gravel, followed by cursing, announced Laura's arrival at the cottage.

Her mad dash into the trees was neither unexpected nor an issue. There was nowhere for her to go, and I had the keys to the boat's engine in my pocket. After being cooped up in the cabin for days, I couldn't blame her seeking her freedom.

There was no freedom to be found on my tiny piece of paradise. The cottage was the one place in the world where I could usually ditch my mask and live as if I wasn't some scarred freak. No-one to gawk at me. No-one to whisper and point. No-one to talk to or expect a reply. The sheep didn't care for me to talk to them anyway.

Night was quickly drawing in, bitter wind sneaking in through the old wooden window frames and creeping around the main room. Dried wood filled the basket near the fire, and I piled some kindling into the grate before adding the aged logs. The strike of the match and the smokey scent of the burning sulphur was like a tonic that soothed me. Fire had destroyed so much, yet it had also brought me my fortune. What other job would someone like me get that didn't require me to wallow in other's pity every fucking day?

The door opened with a scraping sound, and there my pet stood, shivering on the porch.

Laura hesitated on the threshold, glaring at me. Clearly, her afternoon of freedom hadn't tempered her hatred much. Undeniable heat rolled between us on the boat. Her desire had hung heavy in the air and knowing she would have let me touch her had I wanted to was like a drug. The high had hit me without even having slid a hand under her top.

Grabbing a thick woollen blanket, I strode towards her. She didn't flinch when I wrapped the warm cloth around her shoulders and ushered her to the chair by the fire. Landing heavily in the chair, she stared into the quickening fire, the yellow reflected in those big, pretty eyes. Eyes that were rimmed red. Clean tracks marked her cheeks where tears had travelled through dirt.

My ember had had a tough afternoon indeed.

Cuts intersected on her feet, leaving them a bloodied mess. Anger filled me at the sight of them, leaving me wanting to go out and burn every stick and stone that had caused them.

Laura didn't move when I sidled to the kitchen and made a shake, grabbing a first aid kit and a basin of warm, soapy water. The drink sat limp in her hand, condensation pooling against her thigh as I gently pulled her feet into the basin. Kneeling before her, I gently cleaned her feet, washing away blood and grime. There was no fight left in her.

I hoped she hadn't given up. The fire in her was what roused me.

Heat from the hearth seared at my skin while my fingers slid over her broken flesh. I needed to move back and relieve the intense warmth, but I didn't. Holding her in my hands felt like home for the first time since I'd lost them all. Taking her wasn't right, but having her was everything.

After a few minutes of silence, I took her feet from the basin and set them in the centre of a warm towel. She took a sip of the shake and sighed. Sweeping antiseptic over the cleaned cuts didn't even break her from her stupor, nor did wrapping her feet in bandages.

It'll be okay.

I wanted to reassure her, but my words were caged behind my melted lips.

Pink filled her cheeks as she thawed in the cosy room. I cleaned away the basin and medical supplies before grabbing the bags of goodies and handing them to her.

Her eyebrows knitted at the set of navy blue shopping bags.

Opening them up, she peeked inside, before pulling out the items. Toiletries, perfume, underwear, socks and a few sets of clothing piled up on the arm of the seat.

She held up a box of tampons before handing them back over.

'You can keep those for your next victim.'

I took them, arching a brow. I may not have spent a lot of time around women since hitting adulthood, but I knew damn well what periods were.

With a roll of her eyes, she pulled up her sleeve, showing me a tiny lump on her inner arm. 'I have the implant. One sliver of a blessing about this whole mess is that you won't be able to knock me up.'

I blinked at her. I hadn't had any intention of getting her pregnant. Neither had I considered the possibility. Glancing down at her soft stomach, a bolt of need hit me. Imagining her swollen and full with my child gave me a delicious rush. She'd need me.

Laura tucked her arm back into the sleeve as I stood there, salivating over the idea of giving her a part of me she couldn't remove. Growing something together. Her and I, connected, forever.

My dick grew hard and the sensation of possession drew over me like a quilt. I could rip the implant out and fill her with my cum again and again until it seeped out of her.

Her eyes slid to the fire when she saw the expression on my face, her body closing off.

'Thank you for the things,' she said, turning away from me.

Blood coursed through my veins, demanding I rip off the blanket and sink inside her right there on the floor. Nails dug into my palm as I fought off the urge.

Not yet.

A little longer.

Tearing myself away from her, I forced myself into the tiny kitchen. Inhaling deeply through my nostrils, I pushed the overwhelming need back down. It was getting harder and harder to avoid giving in.

Slipping my mask from my mouth, I sloshed cold tap water over my face. Why did Laura affect me so thoroughly? It was like being near her sent my veins into a bubbling fizz, my heart feeling ready to explode. *Everything feeling ready to explode.*

It had to be down to loneliness. Years of only being needed to clean up other people's mess, but never wanted. Not that Laura wanted me. Not yet. But she needed me. For food, shelter and to stave off the isolation.

Like it or not, she'd come back to me. Okay, perhaps it was because she'd had nowhere else to go, but she'd still limped back into my arms all on her own.

It was enough for now.

The water dripped from my chin, washing away the heat coursing through me.

What's your endgame?

The thought prickled at me. I'd never been one to live rashly. Taking Laura was the most unmeasured thing I'd done since my early teens. That and the hatchet in my Uncle's skull. That was a moment of madness built on a lifetime of pain.

Closing my eyes, I let my mind wander. Laura's cheeks pink as she laughed by the sea, holding my hand and pulling me close to her. The laughter of children behind us as gentle waves tickled at their feet. Sweet words whispered in my ear and eyes that filled with joy rather than pain when they met mine.

Days spent in laughter and nights spent in a chorus of desperate moans as she pleads with the gods while I toil between her thighs.

The visceral images in my mind made my stomach knot.

I'd belong. I'd have a family again. Her heart would be my home.

I groaned, abandoning the idea. It would take everything just to get her to tolerate me. The utopia in my mind was nothing but a piece of fiction. Pulling my mask back into place, I left the kitchen.

The fire crackled in the grate, but Laura was no longer where I left her. Her glass sat half-empty on the mantelpiece, but the woollen blanket was gone.

Had she taken the blanket and left? Did she seek shelter on the boat? I tapped my pocket, the engine keys still safely jingling back at me.

A litany of creaks sounded beneath my feet on the ancient staircase. Soft light filtered under the bedroom door, casting its glow over the worn wooden floorboards in the tiny hallway.

Pushing the door open, I saw Laura sat on the edge of the bed cradling a book in her hands. Not just a book, but one of my diaries. Instantly a fiery rage filled my chest. The therapist I'd briefly seen after the accident had suggested I write my feelings down as an outlet since I'd lost my voice. I'd never stopped. Not until the night of my Uncle's death. That was the one thing I hadn't been able to commit to paper.

Laura startled when I walked into the room, slamming the diary closed and shoving it away from her.

'I'm sorry. I shouldn't ha—'

I held up a hand and took a slow breath. She shifted back as I approached the bed, her eyes nothing like the joy filled ones from my imaginings. Maybe her understanding wouldn't be a terrible thing. One person in the world who knew my story would mean I wasn't the apparition I often felt like. When she eventually left me, as everyone did, she'd always know who I was. Who I had been.

Picking up the diary, I slid it back onto the shelf while she stuttered apologies. The oldest, tattiest diary was on the far left, and I slid it out, running my fingers over the dogged cover. Its pages were filled with desperate emotion, stained with tears and blood. Vivid flashbacks of that desperate boy attacked me like wild animals, scratching open wounds I'd long since buried.

Beads of nervous sweat gathered at the back of my neck as I faced Laura.

Her brow crinkled when she spied the tattered book in my hands. I pressed it into her hands before reaching down and tipping her face upwards.

THE BEGINNING, I spelled out on her cheek, her soft skin soothing the anxiety of seeing the book between her fingers.

'You want me to read them?' The way she licked her lips and looked up at me through her thick lashes had me captivated. I nodded.

'And you're not mad at me?'

I shook my head before walking around to the other side of the bed and removing my boots. Her fingers whitened against the diary as she watched me. Laying back against the pillow, I reached for her, pulling her back against my chest.

Laura's body stiffened at the touch, but she remained there.

ONLY READ THEM IN MY ARMS

Her fingers grazed over a bent corner of the cover, the paper rasping beneath her touch. After a few seconds, she nodded, her head bobbing against my chest.

'Okay,' she whispered. 'But only if we have a truce in here. You don't force yourself on me, and I won't push you away while I read. Somewhere where we can just be?'

Already, the warmth of her soft, curved body against mine was divine torture, could I promise that knowing how badly I wanted her?

Then she wriggled against me, making herself more comfortable, her cheek resting sweetly on my chest and the diary balanced against my stomach. The idea of being able to appreciate her, to smell her, watch her, to just indulge in her softness, it was heavenly. For a little while each day I could pretend we were living my day dream. Someone touching me without disgust or fear? And that someone being the angelic faced Laura? Yes. I could do that.

Sliding her hair over one shoulder, I ran my finger over the delicate skin below her ear.

YES

My pulse picked up as she opened the diary and my teenaged scrawl stared back at me.

SIXTEEN

Laura

My head clanged with a thousand danger warnings. Laying on the devil's chest was insane. I'd lost my god-damned mind.

The way he swept his fingers through my hair sent confliction warring through me. The delicate, almost curious stroke of his fingers made tingles dance along my spine. Which left my stomach feeling like I'd swallowed a whole beach full of rocks.

Sighing softly, I focused on the diary. The pages had seen better days, and the text inside harried and rough. The first page held a date nineteen years in the past and a mass of scribblings.

Imran says I have to write my feelings down. If I don't they'll burn me up. Stupid bitch didn't even notice the words she'd used. I've burned enough. The plastic mask and gels I have to have applied so many times a day should be enough for her to think about what she was saying.

My whole family is dead, and everyone keeps refusing to talk about it. They act like me being unable to talk means I don't need answers. Do they know I tried to save May? I tried so hard.

The ink smudged near the bottom of the page, making a few words illegible. I'd cried over enough teen ramblings to recognise a tear splash. My teenage angst filled diaries had been about far more trivial matters, however.

Phoenix's chest rose steadily beneath my cheek, his warmth far more soothing than I should have found it.

'Who's May?' I asked, looking up into his masked face.

LITTLE SISTER

Pain filled those dark eyes of his and I bit my lower lip. Being so close to him, I could see the web of scars filtering up from beneath his t-shirt and snaking up over the side of his face. Imaging him as the kid in the diary made my heart ache.

'How old were you?'

13

The soft traces of his fingers still made me want to pull away from him, but I fought the urge.

So young. He'd tried to save his little sister, from what? A fire? It had to be. Resting my cheek back against his chest, I continued reading.

Uncle Bryan hates me. He doesn't want me. He

told me the only reason he was taking me in was for my parents' insurance money. Five hundred thousand pounds was all they had been worth. Everyone acts like the money should help sooth everything, but I don't want money. I want Mum and Dad and May back.

Her screams fill my head whenever I close my eyes. The way her skin bubbled and peeled when I tried to pull her out from under the beam. It stuck to my own burning fingers. I cried when they'd peeled it away knowing it was all I had left of her. I told her I'd go back for her. That I'd get help.

I hadn't gone back for her.

She died alone, waiting for me.

I daren't breathe. My eyes welled up reading his tortured words. My own family's bloodied bodies flashed into my head and a lump filled my throat.

'It wasn't your fault,' I whispered, trying to suffocate the tears that threatened.

Phoenix didn't respond. He toyed with a strand of my hair and I wallowed in his pain. Our pain. We weren't so different after all.

'Is this why you came back for me?' I asked, my vision blurring the pages in front of me.

YES

I closed the diary, my heart unable to bear any more for the time being. Kneeling up, I face Phoenix, gathering up my courage.

'You don't have to wear your mask around me if you

don't want to. It has to be uncomfortable to wear it all the time.'

He scanned my face, his nostrils flaring as he inhaled deeply.

'We both have our scars. Mine may not be as big, but it isn't pretty.' My stitches itched at the mention of my wound, and I pressed a hand against my hoodie over the spot where I'd been shot by the man I thought I loved.

He slipped his hand up, and peeled the mask away from his face.

I fought the urge to gasp at his mouth, where the skin was melted together, only a tiny space on the far left open. His eyes lowered, clearly waiting for my repulsion.

'You should never have to hide,' I said, placing the diary on the wooden bedside table. For the first moment he'd taken me, I understood in part why. He lived a life hidden away because of the scars he'd had inflicted on him. Inside and out.

And that knowledge could help me.

I didn't doubt he was still dangerous. That he wanted more than a companion. Perhaps, though, he would have a softer side I could appeal to to gain my freedom. Even if it meant submitting to him in the meantime.

Phoenix reached over and turned out the lamp, surrounding us in darkness. An arm wrapped my waist and pulled me down onto the bed, holding me tight to Phoenix's chest.

His nose buried into my hair, making me wince.

DON'T PITY ME, he wrote on my neck with his other hand.

And just like that, I realised underestimating him

wouldn't help me at all. Did I think he'd let me just read in bed without pushing himself on me?

One hand slid up my hoodie, cupping one of my breasts as he groaned softly into my neck. Squeezing my eyes closed, I waited for him to use me, fear making my skin prick up.

Then his grip loosened, his fingers slackening against my nipple. His breathing slowed and his arm grew heavy over my waist.

Phoenix fell asleep, holding me like a fucking teddy bear.

For a moment, knowing he was asleep, I let myself indulge in the feeling of a large, muscled man pressed against my back. I closed my eyes and imagined Massimo hadn't betrayed me. That he'd loved me like I'd longed for him too. That I was a thousand miles away and wrapped up in real love.

SEVENTEEN

Laura

The sickly strawberry taste cloyed against my tongue, the granular texture making me want to puke. How the hell did Phoenix suffer through drinking the shakes all the time? I'd only been having them for what? Ten days or so? Two weeks? God, I was losing track.

I let my mind wander back to the last time I'd seen my house: my family bathed in red and being consumed by orange. Did the police even know I was missing? Did anyone care?

Had Massimo played the devastated fiance? Fooled the world into thinking one of his enemies had taken his beloved woman from him? Or had he simply shrugged and not even given into the pretence that he cared?

Another sip of the wretched liquid fuelled the injustice and anger flowing through me.

Phoenix never drank his shakes in front of me. I'd only see his empty glass to know he consumed anything at all. How many he drank a day to keep his well-muscled body toned, I had no idea.

The way those thick arms had felt holding me against him while he slept washed over me. Warm. Safe. Protective. Yet, he was anything but those things. Phoenix was the enemy. Another Massimo.

Reminding myself was becoming a full time job.

Phoenix stood at the sink, humming to himself as he washed the dishes, his mask still securely around his mouth and nose. Even having shown me the scars inflicted upon him, he preferred to keep it covered.

The third mouthful of the shake came with a lump of unmixed powder exploding against my tongue with its saccharine dry dust. The anger I'd been trying to hide came bubbling up, and I stood, launching the glass at Phoenix. Pinkish liquid splattered up the wall and across the kitchen, shards of glass dispersing amongst the goop.

Phoenix startled, his soapy hands dripping water all over the floor as he turned to survey the mess.

'I can't take any more of that shit,' I said through my teeth, my nostrils flaring with each of my short, furious breaths. 'It's disgusting. I'd rather go and eat the fucking grass with the ponies.'

His brow quirked up at that, and with the memory of him forcing me to clean the boat windows with my tongue still fresh, I wouldn't put it past him to mete out that as punishment.

"I need real food.'

Picking up a dish towel, he dried his hands, all the while scanning the mess in the room. Pink shake dripped from the roof, splashing against the floor with a rhythmic tapping.

My thighs quivered as he strode toward me, my heart leaping into my chest. I glanced at the door, but there was no way I could get to it without him intercepting me. Panic rose with every inch closer he came.

Fuck, what was he going to do?

The chair scraped as I backed up, the wall quickly pressing against my spine. There was a devil in his gaze as he came close. Not anger, but something more wicked.

'I'm sorry,' I muttered, swallowing hard as he closed the space between us. I wasn't, but I hoped it was what he needed to hear.

I flinched as he lifted a hand, but he placed a scarred finger tip on my chest and wrote in slow, steady strokes.

YOU WILL BE

I let out a squeal as he slid his hand up into the back of my hair and used the leverage to pull me forward and roughly bend me over the kitchen table. Strawberry shake squelched beneath my stomach and chest as he pinned me there.

'I'm sorry. Please?'

My pleas fell on deaf ears. Was he going to fuck me? I'd been expecting it every time he was close to me, but so far he'd refrained, even after I made the bargain with him. Maybe I'd finally pushed him too far. I sent a prayer to whatever gods were listening that it would be quick. That he'd be so unused to sex it would be a three stroke and out affair.

I sobbed as he pulled my leggings and underpants down with his free hand. I waited for his intrusion. A minute passed with the table jutting into my hips and my hair held roughly between his fingers.

Nothing.

My breaths shuddered against the shake covered wood as

the cool morning air whispered against my exposed pussy, making my cheeks burn. Was I wet?

Casting the idea from my mind as absurd, I sank back into anger. Why didn't he just do it? Just get it over with.

'Just do it,' I whispered, screwing my eyes shut.

A garbled chuckle sounded. I pursed my lips at the noise. He was finding this funny. What a fucking douche.

I jumped, jarring my hips against the table, when his finger ran over my ass. I had to concentrate on every stroke to figure out what he was writing.

BRATS GET SPANKED

Indignation swept over me.

'I'm not a fucking brat, I'm just sick of your stupid bloody shakes.'

A heavy slap landed on my right ass cheek, a wave of heat following the sharp pain.

'Get off,' I screamed, but his firm hold on my hair stopped me from escaping his grasp.

Another spank followed swiftly, stealing my breath. The painful smacks brought tears to my eyes and fire to my ass.

A few more swats had me writhing against the table, struggling against the mounting pain. It burned like the sun had been buried beneath the skin, angry heat radiating from each mark his hands surely made.

'I'm sorry,' I bubbled, snot mingling with tears and the pieces of my hair which escaped his grasp.

I DON'T BELIEVE YOU

It took every piece of concentration to decipher his letters against my throbbing arse cheeks.

'I am. I'm so sorry. Please, it hurts.'

What hurt more was the awareness of his warm thigh

pressed against my leg, the hardness in his trousers grazing against my hip. The fact that deep down, beneath the rage, something altogether more worrying was brewing. The fact that I knew if he slipped his fingers beneath me, I'd be unable to fight the desire pooling there.

I'd never been spanked, and Phoenix was alighting something inside me that I couldn't ignore.

When another hard swat sent pain whisking through me, I couldn't hold back a desperate little moan. Another spank brought my hip crashing against his hard dick, and I wondered how it would feel filling me. Shame filled me and fought head to head with the lust that his actions wrought.

I wanted it.

And I hated him for it.

My moan made him pause, and my ragged breaths were the only noise in the room.

GOOD GIRL

I sobbed as his praise sent conflicting feelings deep into me. The need to hear him say it, knowing he couldn't, and hatred for talking to me like I was some toy.

His toy.

A shudder darted through me at the delicious wrongness of the thought.

Then my world focused on nothing but one spot as his fingers slid between my legs.

Bliss pulled me into its heady grasp, his fingers finding no resistance with the mess he'd conjured between my thighs.

SO WET he traced against my clit, making me whimper and squirm.

You don't want this.

I screamed the words in my own head, trying to shut out the exquisite touches.

When his fingers stilled, I moved my hips to feel them graze against me, swallowing down the embarrassment of the action.

It's just physiological. It doesn't mean anything.

But fuck it felt good.

The slow strokes as I rocked my hips, sending his fingers sliding against my slickness, made my entire body quiver. My muscles tightened inside me, coiling as if ready to explode and I rode the wave, forgetting to feel shame and chasing a moment's relief from my captivity.

Closing my eyes, I imagined I was somewhere else, with someone else. Imagined it was with a man who adored me. Let myself drift far from the cottage and Phoenix's hands.

So close.

My thighs trembled and I took a gulping breath, ready to tumble into release.

He removed his hand. My hips gyrated against nothing but air and I let out a terrible growl before bursting into frustrated tears.

I'd let him make me want it. And was left with nothing but shame.

He held me fast to the table with his hand in my hair as I cried, leaning over me and using his other finger against my tear stained cheek.

NOT UNTIL YOU BEG

Rage filled me. Rage and desperation. Because I almost begged him right there and then. I wanted to drop to my knees and plead for him to touch me more, and the thought made me want to punch him.

'I'll never beg,' I said through gritted teeth.

WE WILL SEE

Phoenix held me there until the wave of need had passed, leaving me with a sore ass and a bruised ego. Then he stood, adjusted himself, and left.

I'd kill the fucker. Sob story or not.

A little voice in the back of my mind countered with: *But then you can't have his cock.*

Never had I known I could be so furious with myself.

EIGHTEEN

Phoenix

With every stroke of my bow, I could still smell her on my fingers. The lilting, mournful notes filled the late morning air, mingling with the crashing of the waves on the rocks below.

I'd spent so many hours up on the cliff tops as the years had gone by. Usually as an escape from my uncle when he'd had one too many whiskies and decided to let me know how much I owed him for taking me in.

I'd found the ancient violin in one of my hideouts, in a collapsing shed near the cottage. A dusty old trunk tucked beneath a mountain of rotting blankets had hidden it away for god knows how long. It was without a doubt much older than I, but in pretty good shape from what I could tell.

And it was mine.

It was the first thing I'd owned since I lost everything that didn't belong to my uncle. That I hadn't had to silently beg for. I treasured her.

To avoid my uncle taking it away, I only ever played it on the far end of the island, up on the cliff tops. My uncle had grown breathless by that point, and there wasn't a chance in hell he'd climb up there to take it from me.

There were no teachers, and I hadn't been allowed a computer or phone or music books. So I figured it out on my own. Screech by screech. Eventually it started to sound less like a bag of cats being walloped and more like music. Whenever I stumbled back to the cottage, tired and hungry, my fingertips would be swollen from pressing on the strings.

Never had any moment of playing been quite so sweet as with the scent of my angry little ember wafting between the notes.

Settling into a long, woeful Scottish melody, I played into the light morning wind. The sea stretched out before me and I was alone in my piece until a soft voice broke the quiet.

Without missing a note, I turned to see Laura sitting on a moss covered stump, her eyes glazed as she stared out over the ocean. Her lips moved as though enchanted, the beautiful sound tumbling from them despite her looking a thousand miles away.

She knew the song I played, so I continued it for her, the music wrapping around her silken words and filling the area around us with delight. I'd never been able to sing along with the music. When I'd finally gotten access to the internet after my uncle was dead, I'd long given up hope of ever being able to use my mouth. It had been too long. My uncle had long told me that. There was nothing to be done for me.

Laura's eyes sparkled with tears as her voice cracked mid verse. It was like a dagger to the gut. Was she crying because I'd touched her? She'd been so wet, her body crying out for more. I knew she was stuck with me, but there was something there between us, I could feel it. I just needed her to feel it too.

Sweat broke out on my forehead as I played my violin harder filling the gap left by her cessation of singing. A soft whicker tore my eyes from her as the wild ponies loitered at the edge of the plateau. They'd often come to hear me play, but had always been too skittish to be my friends. No matter how badly I'd have loved for them to be.

One broke from the group and lowered its head, treading over the grass to where Laura sat. I watched, mesmerised, as it gave me a cautious look before nuzzling gently at her tear streaked face.

Of course she'd bewitched them like she'd bewitched me. We were all powerless beneath her perfection.

Laura let out a giggle as his brown snout tickled at her, her fingers coming up to tenderly stroke at his nose.

Jealousy filled my stomach, and I pulled my violin down to my side, watching as they both betrayed me with their intimacy.

I'd longed for both of them to react to me with the soft, sweetness in which they embraced. Yet neither had deigned to see me worthy.

It was ridiculous to be jealous of a pony, or of it giving its attention to Laura, but it was yet another rejection.

Still, as much as it pained me to see them making friends without me, it was still a perfect vision. My girl being so tender was a joy to witness, even if it was for a beast more fair than I. She deserved love, and why would she choose to have it from me? A deformed creep who'd stolen her away in the night. A monster who wanted to consume her every breath.

A nothing.

Sure, I had money. Maybe that would be enough if she knew about how lucrative my job was, but I wanted to be wanted. To have her whisper my name into the sheets at night, and laugh with me over the dinner table. To hear her beg for my touch so prettily in the depths of night.

I should let her go.
I can't.

NINETEEN

Laura

The music had drawn me toward him. Eerie, sad notes twisting their way through the heather and pulling me in. When Phoenix picked up that damn violin he may as well have been a siren, luring me to disaster. Despite my anger from him tanning my arse and then leaving me wanting more, I struggled to stay away.

The ponies had lingered near him, curious but wary. Muffin, as I'd named the scruffy little pony with the dark brown dots – like a chocolate chip muffin – had come over and nuzzled into me.

Shortly after, Phoenix's violin screeched to a halt and he stalked off down the hill with his arms tensing, his fingers white around the violin's neck.

My shoulders relaxed as he departed and I threaded my fingers into Muffin's matted mane.

'What am I going to do?' I asked the pony. 'I'm stuck

here, just like you. But I don't belong here. I need to get away.'

Muffin whickered into my shoulder as I ran my hands down over his neck, giving him a jolly good scratch.

'Thing is, he touched me. And it felt like how I'd always wished it would. Not with him, obviously, but when I lay in bed and dreamed of Massimo. Phoenix makes me want it. And I despise it. I don't want to want his touch.'

I sighed and stood, brushing dry dirt from the back of my clothes, watching as little flecks of grass drifted down to the ground. The raging fire his hands had left burning on my ass cheeks had dulled to a soft ache. I screwed my face up at the thought of being bent over with him chastising me. Who did he think he was?

'And why did it make me wet?' I asked Muffin, who ducked his head down to munch on a patch of clover near my feet.

I needed to get out. But how? Could I take the boat? Old Bess couldn't be that difficult to man, right? Even if I could just get it far enough out to sea that Phoenix couldn't swim out and sent out some kind of mayday signal.

It wasn't a concrete plan, but it was the best I had.

I just needed a way to get the keys. Phoenix almost always kept them on him. He needed to be distracted. Distracted and trusting.

Maybe I needed to play along with his game. Men usually slept like the dead after a good lay. I could suck it up long enough to get him knackered and then take the keys from discarded trousers, right?

Fuck, if I played it right, made him as desperate as he was trying to make me, I could have the keys by nightfall.

'You wouldn't be mad, would you Muffin? You'd understand my leaving? I need to get home. Tell the police about Massimo, and my family, and Phoenix. Maybe I could come back for you when he's in jail. Take you home with me.' I sighed as tears pricked in the corners of my eyes. 'Not that I have a home anymore.'

Muffin didn't seem to mind either way.

A light rain smattered the grimy old cottage windows, the pitter patter a soothing companion as I read Phoenix's teenaged scrawl. He may have set the rule that I had to only read it in his arms, but what was he going to do? Spank me again?

The delicious thrill that spread out from between my thighs made me scowl. Stupid, treacherous vagina. *Who's side are you even on?*

Refocusing on the diary, I read on through a particularly angry entry.

> *I don't know if he's ever going to take me back to the doctors. We've been on the boat for so long. Has everyone forgotten about me? Sometimes I wonder if I ever even existed. May, Mum and Dad feel like a dream. I keep trying to picture their faces, but they are getting foggier every day. I wish*

I had some photos. Something of us all together. I miss them so much.

I miss everything. I miss my friends, my school, even the nights arguing with Mum about eating my veggies. I'd give anything to have her back. And my mouth back.

Uncle let me starve for a bit when I refused to drink the awful pink shakes. When my hip bones started sticking out he forced the shakes into the hole I have left in my mouth. It would make me vomit, and then I have no option but to swallow the soured shakes back down when I couldn't spit them out.

I hate him.

I HATE the shakes.

But I take them to avoid having him sit on my chest and choke me with them. One day I'll be strong enough to kill him. I'll sit on his chest and drown him in the fucking vile liquid. Then I'll go home. Find someone who cares.

The word cares was blemished with a years old teardrop, the ink spreading around the word in a blurry black smudge.

Phoenix hated the shakes as much as I did. He'd had nothing else to eat for years.

A noise in the doorway had me startle upright, closing the book.

Time for operation make him come, then steal the keys.

I wanted to gag at the thought of him anywhere near me,

but I'd done worse things with people who didn't even know my clit seemed to exist. At least if I closed my eyes, I might be able to get that itch scratched before I left him in the dust.

Phoenix climbed onto the bed, pulling me and the diary into his arms.

Operation play it sweet, Laura. You can do it.

'I'm sorry about this morning, I shouldn't have thrown the glass.' I tapped the diary before looking over my shoulders. The half mask covered his lower face, but his intense eyes met my glance. 'I didn't realise how much you hated them too. I'm so sorry.'

His fingers danced over my hip, dragging my focus to their gentle touch.

IT'S OKAY

My plan to seduce him caught inside me, the idea too ridiculous when he was pressed all up against me. I didn't want him to fuck me. I definitely didn't want him in my mouth. Would tossing him off do the trick?

Reaching around me, he plucked the diary from my hands and placed it on the bedside table before turning off the light.

Pitch darkness enveloped us, making me painfully aware of the heat of his body against mine. I screwed my eyes shut as he shifted, a soft thump landing on the floor as he stripped off his clothing.

No. No. No. I wasn't ready.

Tension hardened my every muscle when he wrapped his naked form around me, pulling me under the covers against him.

At least he left my t-shirt and shorts on.

After a few minutes wrapped in his embrace, I began to relax. He was just holding me like he had the previous night.

Maybe he doesn't even want you. No one does.

The insidious thought bounded around my head, utterly unwelcome. I didn't want him to want me. Not really. I'd just spent so many years watching everyone else find men who couldn't keep their hands off of my friends. Worshipping them. Doing anything for a grain of their attention. I'd always only been the other friend. The one they brought a mate along to the double date for. The one getting a pity fuck at the end of the night because it was better than nothing else.

Not even the scarred, lonely man who took me was desperate enough to want me.

The two ideas warred in my head. Wanting to be wanted, and wanting to be a million miles from Phoenix.

Had he fallen asleep?

I listened to his breathing, trying to decide if he'd settled into the familiar pattern of sleep.

His hand moved against my hip, pulling me backward. Something large and hard nudged against my ass, making me flinch. Good lord. Phoenix arched against me, the head of his naked cock rubbing against my arse.

I ignored it entirely.

Let the sick fuck hump me all he liked.

His breath was hot against my neck, his masked face grazing the flesh there as he picked up the pace, using me like a pillow to grind.

Ignoring him was hard enough, but possible, until he hauled one of my legs up over his hips and pressed his solid dick against my panties. Shame burned in my cheeks when he dragged the word WET across my stomach with his fingers.

With each arch of his hips, the head of his cock pressed up and over my clit, sending spirals of pleasure dancing through me.

Fuck.

The action was salacious. Being ridden like a dog humping a leg, and yet I couldn't ignore the growing need each stroke fuelled within me. One large hand pressed against the spot right above my pussy, eliciting even more sensation.

Pain erupted as I bit down on my lip, trying to stifle the moans threatening to overwhelm me. Phoenix's earthy smell, like fresh grass and autumn rain, filled my nostrils with every laboured pant I took.

I wouldn't give in. Wouldn't give him what he wanted. I'd get his keys another way.

'Oh god,' I whimpered when he circled my clit between the ongoing sliding of his cock against my panties. Sweat slicked between us, hot and dewy beneath the darkness. Using his fingers beneath my panties, he spread me wide, nudging his cock over my clit with precise little thrusts.

A gasp ripped from me, my thighs trembling. I waited to fall over the edge. Waited for him to pull my panties to the side and thrust that cock of his deep inside me. Waited. Waited. Waited.

He held me there with ease, not giving me enough to send me tumbling, but neither letting up on the onslaught against my clit.

'Just fuck me,' I panted, fury and need overriding any sense of self preservation.

BEG he wrote against my clit with those fucking fingers.

I wanted to. I really did.

Every single part of my body was strung as tightly as his

violin, his cock like his bow, playing me so expertly. He'd mastered my flesh so easily. All I had left was my mind.

Giving in wasn't an option.

'Never,' I gasped.

His hips stilled, and I cursed myself in my head. I waited for him to move. To let me go and pull away. Instead he held me there against him, his cock nestled between my pussy lips, my wet panties all bunched up between us and his fingers still pressing against my clit.

I was awake long after he fell asleep, rage burning me to a crisp.

TWENTY

Phoenix

The wind whipped at my bare shoulders while the sun peeked up over the eastern horizon. A layer of salty sweat covered my skin, mingling with the light dusting of rain the clearing mists had brought.

My muscles ached with every chop of my axe, my biceps protesting at every jarring bite into the logs. I'd needed something to distract me from Laura.

I'd woken up still entangled with her and my obsession had exploded before I'd even opened my eyes. The feel of her soft, warm skin against me. The way her sweet breaths tickled at the gap between my shoulder and my neck where she lay pressed against me. My cock hard against her hip and my fingers still tangled up in her moist panties.

Fuck me.

I needed her more than I needed to fucking breathe.

It took every single fibre of my being to drag myself away

from her. To pull on trousers and slip away from her sweet, soft skin.

As I slid out from beneath her, her jutting hip bone grazed me and threw back to my time on the hunger strike when I was a teen. My time before I'd accepted the revolting shakes were my new normal.

My beautiful girl was suffering. Wasting away. I needed to find her food she'd actually eat. The last time I'd run down to the shops with a pocketful of change to buy something to eat had been far too long ago. I couldn't even remember it. More than likely I'd had May trailing me, pestering me to buy her some penny sweets. I'd have likely sighed about her having to come with me, but scooped her up in my arms when we reached the counter like I always did to pick the paper bag that looked the most full.

Shaking the memory away at the physical hurt it wrought, I heaved the axe into another log, my breath fogging in front of me. I kept going until the pile of logs were fully split into log burner sized pieces. My chest rose in exhausted pants while I leant against the cool stone walls of the cottage.

A movement inside caught my eye.

Laura was inside the little bathroom, stripping off the shorty underwear I'd ground against the previous night. She stood looking into the little mirror above the sink, scraping a brush through her hair, before reaching over and turning the metal knob which sent water cascading down into the bathtub.

Oh sweet Laura... You need to give in and beg.

It was killing me to taunt her and deny myself her screams of pleasure. I needed them almost as badly as she did. She still fought my touch, her body cried out for it with every torturous little whimper she gave.

What I'd do to have her look up at me with those big doe eyes and beg for me to make her come. To hear my name in a strangled cry tumbling from her lips.

She bent over to swish the water in the tub, giving me a spectacular view of her arse and the still swollen pink lips peeking out between her soft thighs. I wanted to tear open my stupid scarred lips and bite her. To lick her tears from her cheeks after she begged me so prettily for more. To redden her skin until it glowed before thrusting into the one place I was sure would feel like home.

What had started as a stupid, reckless moment of madness was quickly turning into a deep obsession.

My Laura.

My darkest craving.

She stood and stretched before stepping into the water, sinking into it with a silent sigh. I should get her bubbles. Then she could be like one of those women on TV. I'd never bothered with them just for me.

Laura rested back and lifted a leg, running her fingers over it before reaching over the edge of the bath to one of the bags I'd gotten for her. She pulled out one of the safety razors and worked it over her leg in slow, careful strokes.

My pretty brat preening for me.

She had to be.

There was no way she was shaving to impress the fucking pony.

Watching her had my dick pressing at the front of my trousers, desperate to break free. I rubbed my hand against it, remembering the heat between her thighs. Every little tremor deep in her cunt had emanated outward and twitched against the head of my cock. Sinking into her had been the only thing on my mind, how her hot, wet, heat would have welcomed me.

Pulling my cock free, I stroked down its length, shuddering while I stared at my girl. Her tits were shiny with the bath water and gleaming in the low light. I wanted to pinch the dark pink nipples that sat just above the water, twist them until tears sprung in her eyes.

A strangled noise made its way up my throat. Focusing my hand on the head of my cock, I imagined climbing into the bath and sinking my hips to her mouth, watching those plump lips swallowing me down. Would she be a good girl and take it all? Or would I have to coax each inch into her, delighting in every cough and gag?

My balls tensed when she put down the razor and slipped a hand between her thighs.

Oh my little spark, you know your fingers aren't going to do what mine will.

I knew because my hand was a poor replacement for the feel of her body writhing against me.

Her head tipped back as she pressed her fingers into her cunt. I wanted to chop every one of them off with my axe just so I could be the only one who could please her.

Mine.

All fucking mine.

The world tilted as I fucked my fist, watching Laura trying to elicit the same feelings I'd teased out of her. My breath caught when I came, hot cum squelching between my fingers with every rough stroke of my hand. I kept going until the sensitivity was too much, determined to leak every drop for my sweet Laura.

The window fogged where my breath heated it, and Laura glanced up, shrieking before grabbing a towel from the rail and pulling it into the bath to cover herself up.

I laughed behind my broken mouth.

If only she'd seen what I'd done for her.

I held up my hand, her eyes widening at the white liquid dripping from my fingers.

Next time, it'd be inside her.

TWENTY-ONE

Laura

Muffin trailed after me, both of us stepping over the exposed rocks as we made our way to the cottage. The gentle clop of his hooves made my shoulders relax, his nearness like a soothing balm.

The bathroom window glinted in the low evening sun, reminding me of Phoenix watching me bathing. After him being pressed up against me all night, his fingers thrust into my underwear, him watching me shouldn't have been a shock. The watching wasn't even the worst of it. He'd held up his hand and shown me exactly what he'd been doing.

Disgusting.

And maybe just a little bit hot.

If a man had ever been so overcome at the sight of me he needed to masturbate, I'd certainly never been privy to the information. Didn't he see my imperfections? It was one thing to want a warm body in the dark of night, but a whole other to see them in the light of day and touch yourself.

God dammit, Laura, you're fucking crazy. He's a psycho.

Or maybe I was. Because seeing his cum dripping from his fingers made me wish I could lick it off. Only for one insane moment, but the thought had been there.

It was like being near him possessed me with some sort of carnal demon. I wasn't like that.

I was...

Well. Who was I? Even if I made it home I wouldn't be the woman who my mother dragged reluctantly into society life. There would be no parties to arrange, no family to try and impress. No fiance. Nowhere to call home. I'd likely be met with pity. If what Massimo said was true, there was no money left either in my family coffers. I'd need to find a job. To start over.

Maybe that wouldn't be the worst thing.

Maybe I could be something I was proud of. What if I could rise from tragedy and turn it into a life I loved.

That life was like a fog. There were no solid shapes to it. My upbringing had focussed entirely on one future. A future that didn't even fit around me. One I was being wedged into. If I were to start again on my own, where would I even begin?

Muffin and I reached the cottage, and I giggled as he tried to nose his way into the kitchen.

'There's nothing in there for you, buddy. I don't think you want the strawberry shakes.' I scratched the side of Muffin's neck before directing him to a particularly overgrown patch of grass near the door.

Silence greeted me indoors. Most of the day I'd spent up on the clifftop dreaming about escaping the stupid little island in between short bursts of remembering the way Phoenix's scarred fingers felt between my thighs. I sung to the ponies and threw pebbles into the ocean. Anything but being stuck in the tiny cottage with *him*.

The bedroom was empty, the bedding still crumpled where I'd left it. He wasn't in the bathroom, nor anywhere around the cottage exterior.

Panic started to make me sweat. Where was he hiding? Was it some sort of game to freak me out?

My eyes grazed over the shoreline, following the beach to the dock.

The empty dock.

Holy shit.

Phoenix had abandoned me!

My breath snagged in my chest while my legs turned to jelly beneath me.

It was one thing to be captive on the island while planning my escape, but to be abandoned there alone suffocated me with terror.

The cottage wall met my back as I stumbled over the patchy grass, a sob ripping from my throat.

What if he didn't come back?

There was no way I could survive on the shakes forever. There weren't enough for more than a few weeks.

Muffin blinked at me.

'Don't worry, I'm not going to eat you,' I snivelled, trying to calm my breathing. The pony tipped his head up and let out a whinny before going back to his grass. 'At least you won't run out of food. Maybe I'll end up joining you on a grass diet.'

I slid to my ass and sat there until the night shoved the day below the horizon and my skin grew so cold it began to ache. No lights appeared on the darkening sea.

You should be happy. He's gone. Another boat might come along and set you free.

But what if they didn't. What if someone worse than Phoenix found me? He was far from a saint, but he'd looked after me in his own way. He'd held off on fucking me despite our agreement. He wanted me to want it.

It wasn't exactly gentlemanly behaviour, but it could have been much worse.

With my limbs burning from the chill, I made my way indoors with an armful of firewood.

By the time I had the log burner going, and a cup of awful strawberry shite to drink, I was cursing Phoenix all over again.

He hadn't even left a fucking note.

What a monumental prick.

If he ever dared show his face, I'd be ready for him. He'd regret ever picking me out of that fire.

TWENTY-TWO

Phoenix

My heart beat hard in my chest with every jostling person who bumped into me. It beat even harder at the ones who's eyes widened as they took me in before giving me a wide berth.

The half face mask didn't cover all of my scars, and the staring was something I'd had to grow used to. For most of my life, since the fire, I tried to avoid crowded spaces as much as possible.

It would be worth it.

For Laura.

The supermarket's lights glared above me, and row after row of colourful items stretched out seemingly endlessly. A tremble made my fingers quake when I reached out for one of the packets, picking it up and feeling the squishy contents within. The gummy worms weren't at all nutritious. A waste of money, really. Frivolous. *Perfect.*

Throwing the jellied sweets into the trolley began an

avalanche of food stuffs. Things I remembered loving from my childhood, like chocolate mice and tiny icing covered biscuits. Packet after packet of items I'd never even heard of but would love to taste. Pizza flavoured crisps. Wine flavoured sweets. BBQ ramen noodles.

After almost an hour and a stuffed trolley, I reined myself in. The trolley was teeming with nothing but junk food, and my fiery little ember would need some real food. Never in my life had I had to actually shop and cook actual meals.

The cool pack of burgers I picked up chilled the tips of my fingers as I scanned the back. Fry until cooked through. I could do that for her. My mouth watered at the distant memory of melted cheese and seasoned patties my dad would cook on the barbeque in the summer.

Damn. I'd have loved to taste even one more bite.

Almost as much as I longed to taste Laura.

Being near her drove me insane. The way her nose scrunched in distaste at the shakes made my heart want to explode in my chest. The little snores she gave off in the night. Her soft hair clinging to my chest in the middle of the night when she was too deep in the unconscious to remember to be mad at me. When she'd sung along to my violin I'd been hit with a hundred more poisoned darts that inflamed my desire for her a thousand-fold. I wanted to hear her cry my name out in that pretty sing-song voice of hers.

My thumb was digging into the minced beef patties through the cellophane as I lost myself in Laura. The supermarket dimmed, so inconsequential compared to even the smallest thought of her.

I had to make her mine.

To show her I would worship her like no other man ever would.

To torment her body in ways that would leave her never wanting to be anywhere but at my feet.

Someone cleared their throat, dragging me right back into the supermarket with a sharp bump. The elderly woman glanced down at my crotch, her eyes widening.

Shit.

The thoughts of Laura on her knees had made me hard, and to the other patrons it must have looked every bit like I had a chub on for fucking hamburgers.

I tossed the pack of burgers into the cart before winking at the old woman and walking past her, very much trying to ignore the glances from others at my crotch.

After piling some vegetables and fruit into the cart, I stopped next to a basket of the shiniest, reddest apples I'd ever seen. Would Laura like them?

That damned pony would.

And Laura liked the pony.

And I wanted to make her smile so fucking badly.

With a sigh, I scooped an armful of the apples up and dumped them into the cart.

Stupid bloody pony better at least let me pet him.

Or Laura might beg me to pet her...

My muscles spasmed as I wrangled the stuffed carrier bags into the cottage. The birds chittered above the front door in their early morning sing-song, adding to the blissful quiet of the day. Having been back in the busyness of the real world always made me appreciate the isolation of the island. However hard it had been being stuck there with my uncle, at least there was no one to stare at my ugly, deformed face. No gasps or children pointing. No mothers pulling toddlers out of my path or people asking what happened.

At least on the island it was only me.

And Laura, now.

Flexing my fingers to stretch out the cramp from the bag's indents, I walked through to the sitting room. Laura's pretty face pressed against her arm in the worn old armchair, her mouth open a little. Her breath was soft against the woollen blanket that covered her.

My sweet girl hadn't been able to go to bed without me. A bloom of pleasure filtered through me. I stepped closer to her sleeping form and slowly dragged my thumb over her bottom lip.

What I'd give to kiss you.

To have lips to press against yours. To be able to feel your breath against my tongue. To swallow down every little gasp.

The temptation to thrust my thumb into the heat of her mouth pulled at me. I had no doubt she could bring me to my knees with that mouth if she wanted to. I may be waiting for her to beg, but if I could talk, I'd throw myself at her goddamned feet and plead for the slightest ounce of her attention.

My pulse thundered in my chest. Standing there at a

precipice. Wanting horribly to wake her and make her writhe against my hand.

Closing my eyes, I sighed.

Waking her up with food might at least make her hate me a little less.

The old range cooker hadn't been switched on since my uncle had stopped needing to eat. I hadn't even considered getting gas.

Damn it.

I took the pack of bacon I'd opened outside along with an old frying pan and set them aside while I made a ring of stones on the grass. The wood scraped at my fingers, sharp little daggers cutting into me while I stacked them in the ring.

The fire took easily when I held a match to the thinner pieces of kindling I'd piled at the bottom of the stack. Soon orange flames crackled up, and my eyes glazed over while I waited for them to peak. The sea lapped at the shore, the minutes passing glacially slow while the wood burned black, glowing embers soon replacing the bright flames.

The bacon fat sizzled in the pan, spitting and bubbling in the heat.

Fuck, it smelled delicious.

Would Laura like it crispy? Or soft?

My mouth watered.

'You came back.' I startled at the voice, turning to nod at Laura.

'I can't believe you left me here on my own! What kind of absolutely insane fucker...' Laura stopped mid-sentence, her expression changing when she caught sight of the bacon. 'Is that bacon?'

I gave another nod, moving aside as she came to stand beside me, her eyes like saucers.

'Did you go shopping? For me?'

I glanced at her face, seeing sleepy eyes glittering. The fire it ignited in me was more fierce than any of the thousands I'd lit.

Reaching out, I took her hand, upturning her palm.

YES

Laura snatched it back before clearing her throat.

'Thank you,' she whispered.

Feeling awkward at her mixed reaction, I walked inside and buttered a white bread roll.

Laura sat next to the fire, her eyes fixed on the frying pan.

The minute I scooped the hot bacon into the bun, she all but snatched it out of my fingers, moaning as she took a bite.

Her eyes rolled backward, and there I was, jealous of a fucking sandwich. Grease leaked out over her fingers as she chewed, and I desperately wanted to lick them clean.

Fuck my stupid fucking mouth.

After swallowing down a few more bites, Laura smiled shyly at me before licking her fingers clean.

My poor heart nearly stopped at the way her tongue wrapped round the digits.

'I don't think I've ever tasted anything so delicious,' she said. Her eyes flicked to my mask, and then back down to her food, a frown crossing her perfect lips. 'I'm sorry. I was so hungry I didn't even think about how it must feel for you. You hate the shakes too.'

I shrugged, and lifted a hand indicating she should keep eating. Moving closer, I sat beside her and placed a finger on her exposed thigh.

THERE'S NO NEED FOR US BOTH TO SUFFER

'Thank you.' She nibbled at the sandwich. 'I thought you'd left me here. It scared me.'

I spelled out sorry on the soft skin of her thigh.

'I don't know what to do. I hate you. You were watching me. You've been touching me. And I hate that it feels good.'

Guilt hit my chest. Of course she didn't want someone like me touching her.

'Why do you even want me here? Is it because you've never had sex? If we have sex will you let me go?'

No, sweet girl. I can never let you go.

I shook my head.

'But why?' Her voice rose to a higher pitch.

OBSESSED WITH YOU

Her breath hitched, and she scrutinised my face with those big doe eyes.

'Why though? You don't even know me.'

I lifted one of her hands and pressed it against my chest. It wasn't about knowing. It was a feeling. The moment I saw her in the burning room, there was something that told me she was supposed to be with me. To be mine.

Her eyes focused on mine, my pulse thudding against her palm with the closeness of her. Then her brow creased and she pulled her palm away.

Awkwardness settled over us like a stifling blanket.

'Did you buy anything else?' she asked, focusing on the burning logs.

EVERYTHING

A smile turned up the corner of her mouth as I traced the word on her skin.

EVEN APPLES

Her eyebrow quirked up as she made sense of my spelling.

'Apples?'

PONY

Softness infused her features and gave me an injection of pleasure of a whole different kind.

'I've called him Muffin. Thank you. It was... sweet... for you to think of him.'

I cleared my throat and stood, conflicting feelings swarming through me. She didn't want to be with me. I didn't want to be without her.

With the awkward exchange playing over in my mind, I left the cottage, seeking a distraction. How could I make Laura see past the scarred face and the fact I'd taken her?

TWENTY-THREE

Laura

Phoenix wasn't beside me when I awoke, and hadn't touched me as he slept next to me either.

Instead of the relief I should have felt, I wondered what had changed.

He'd told me he was obsessed with me, but while I'd laid next to him and awaited the pressure of his warm arms wrapping around me, he'd rolled over and just slept.

You don't want him.

But you enjoyed being wanted.

Letting out a groan, I flopped myself back onto the pillow. It wasn't some twisted fairytale. What did I think would happen? That I could fall in love with the monster who took me and he'd suddenly turn into a prince? No. My prince had shot me in the chest and called a monster to burn me.

What a joke.

My life had been pointless. All those lessons in etiquette

and social class, and I was stuck with Phoenix and Muffin in the back of beyond. Everything was for nothing.

And yet, there was peace in the loss too.

My days were empty, but there was no social pressure either. No one to live up to or impress.

Phoenix burst through the door, making me shriek. His mask covered his lower face, but delight lit up his eyes. If I hadn't known what lay beneath the mask, I'd have thought he was smiling.

'What is it?' I asked, curiosity piquing my interest.

He crossed the room and grabbed my hand, all but pulling me out of the bed. A chill hit my naked legs as he dragged me along, down the stairs and out into the misty morning.

'Phoenix! I'm not even dressed. What are you doing?'

For the first time I was glad there were no neighbours to see me out in a t-shirt and underpants.

We stopped a few minutes from the cottage, where Muffin stood.

'Oh hey boy,' I said, reaching out to give his neck a scratch.

Phoenix tapped on my arm before taking an apple from his pocket. Using his bare hands, he twisted it in half before offering a piece to the pony.

I watched, confused by his excitement.

Muffin took the apple from his fingers, before accepting a petting. Phoenix looked up at me, his fingers lost in the shaggy ponies soft fur.

Realisation hit.

All his time on the island, and he'd never touched the ponies?

'He never let you pet him before?' I asked, stepping closer and running my fingers through Muffin's mane. The pony nudged at Phoenix's other hand, encouraging him to hand over the other half of the apple.

Phoenix shook his head before signalling to his face.

'You thought it was because of your scars?'

He nodded.

'It's more likely because you storm about looking like you're ready to punch people in the face at the drop of a hat. Animals can sense it. I'm not sure they care much about scars.'

Phoenix's fingers grazed over the edge of his mask, skimming his scarred cheek and for a moment I saw the boy from the diaries. The fear, the loneliness, the kid who lost everything. A reflection of me. Lost and alone. Alone, but together.

The urge to hug him swept me, the hair on my arms lifting at the thought of willingly embracing him. Swallowing hard, I thrust the urge away, clenching my fingernails into my palms.

Being lonely wasn't a reason to give into him. He took me. Stole me away.

He is the enemy.

'I need to go shower,' I said, taking an awkward step backward. Phoenix's fingers stilled on Muffin's soft nose and he gave a nod. Knowing how excited he'd been, it was like kicking a bloody puppy.

Cheese bubbled out of the edge of my sandwich as it toasted. The crisp, browning bread made my mouth water and it couldn't cook fast enough.

My stomach rumbled angrily, roiling with each passing moment.

Finally, I swept it out of the pan, piercing it with a fork and moving it onto my waiting plate.

Phoenix sat on the rock beside me, his pink-filled glass clenched in his hand.

'I'm sorry you have to keep drinking that stuff.'

Phoenix shrugged, turning away as he slipped the straw beneath his mask. The fire light flickered over his tightly muscled forearms and I swallowed hard, trying to push the thought of them wrapped around me away.

There were too little distractions on the island. Bar Muffin, it was Phoenix and I. Days spent awkward and then nights with him driving me to the point of wanting to beg for his touch. My brain felt utterly scrambled.

I wanted to push him off of the cliff top as much as I wanted him to just take what he demanded of me. He made me promise to give him what he wanted, and I had expected him to just want to use me. But he wanted more. He wanted my consent. He wanted me to need it.

I couldn't let myself go there.

He stole me from my life, no matter how shattered it had become. Refusing to ask for it was the only control I had left.

The hot toasted edge of the sandwich crunched between my fingers. Tearing off a chunk, I slipped it into my mouth, closing my eyes at the rich, creamy bubbling cheese. Back home I'd eaten from top chefs menus, at the most elite parties and restaurants, yet never had I tasted something that hit the spot so thoroughly.

Birds fought over the crust I tossed near the edge of the water. Phoenix finished his shake and turned back toward the fire, mask firmly in place.

Silence enveloped us. There was so much quiet. Too much.

'Did you know we were supposed to marry?'

Phoenix shook his head.

'Massimo and I. It was the eve of our wedding. I was so fucking excited. It was pathetic. At first I hadn't even wanted to marry him, but he sent me all these letters which completely won me over.'

Phoenix watched me as I spoke, his gaze palpable on the side of my face while I stared at the fire.

'They were so sweet, full of romance and heat. God, I was such an idiot. It was nothing but a business deal to him. For so many nights I'd pored over his letters, analysing every word, committing them to memory. I thought I was finally going to have someone who adored me, but I was nothing to him.'

My voice cracked as I spoke, my lap covered in crumbs from tearing my sandwich into tiny pieces.

'How could I have believed he'd feel like that about me? He's handsome, and wealthy, and could have any woman he wanted. I was utterly deluded. He took everything from me, and for what? More money? To save face when my father screwed him over.'

Rage flowed through me as I babbled.

Scarred fingers grazed over my leg, and it took everything to focus in on the little letters Phoenix drew there.

You're perfect.

He didn't deserve you.

I scoffed and moved away from him, scraping my leg on the sharp edge of one of the rocks.

'Fuck,' I hissed through my teeth as a line of red welled from the scrape. Blood dripped as I jumped up.

Phoenix didn't pause, he stood, placing his glass down and scooped me up in his arms.

'I can walk,' I said in a meek voice. I didn't want him to carry me, but having his arms wrapped around me was a balm I sorely needed. How long had it been since I'd had a hug?

Too long.

Warmth from his chest seeped into me. He traversed his way to the cottage and ducked us through the door. When he deposited me on the kitchen table, I almost broke and begged him to keep holding me. I urged on the last bit of will power I had, and pushed the desperation for human touch back down.

Phoenix rooted through the cabinets until he found an ancient looking green box. It clanked with a metallic thud as he placed it down on the counter beside me.

Flipping open the lid revealed a little stash of medical supplies. He picked up a bottle of antiseptic and some cotton pads and knelt between my legs, gently cupping the back of my injured calf.

He wiped my cut with a slow, steady sweep of the cotton, making me wince. The antiseptic stung, and I bit down on my lower lip to stop me from cursing at him.

He blinked up at me through dark lashes, reaching for a large sticking plaster from the tin.

God, a woman could lose herself entirely in those dark eyes. They were like voids that screamed of pain and loneliness, but ringed with so much promise too. Eyes of two sides, like Jekyll and Hyde. A monster and a saviour all in one twisted shell.

'I never thanked you,' I said, 'For fixing me after Massimo shot me.'

Phoenix's jaw flinched beneath the mask, the edges flaring outward.

DON'T WANT TO HEAR HIS NAME ON YOUR LIPS.

His fingers skimmed up toward my thighs as he wrote on my skin, pushing them apart.

His mask was level with my pussy, the heat from his breath evident against my shorts.

Holding my breath, I waited to see what he'd do.

Phoenix pressed his face against me, the pressure instantly igniting my need for his touch. But there was no way he could go down on me, not with his scarred mouth.

Gripping his hands around my ass, he pulled me forward to the edge of the counter and buried his face between my thighs. Phoenix inhaled deeply through his nose, my face burning. I didn't have time to worry about him smelling me though. He ground his face into me, using his chin and face to bring a desperate moan tumbling from my lips.

I tried to resist. To keep still and pretend like it did nothing for me, but the sheer filthiness of him rubbing his face against me had me trembling against the counter within minutes. When he hummed with pleasure, it was too much to bear.

Arching my hips, I rode his face, losing all composure. Heat built in my groin, pressure increasing with each graze of his masked face. My clit throbbed, and I wanted to tear my fucking clothes off and beg him to fuck me right there.

I wanted more.

No, I needed more.

'Phoenix,' I moaned, my voice barely a croak.

My utterance made his whole body stiffen as he panted against my wet shorts. His eyes darkened and he stood, pulling me to my feet.

I squeaked at the sudden movement, already missing his face between my legs, air cooling the fire there without him.

He drove his fingers into my hair, tipping my head back and forcing me to look into his face.

BEG

He wrote the word against my neck, my pulse beating beneath his fingers. My stomach lurched at the demand, my hackles raising at his insistence on making me ask for it.

'No.'

His eyebrows creased before he released me from his grip and made space between us.

'I won't beg for it. Never.' My words were harsh, but still didn't cover the need beneath them.

He grabbed a marker from a pot on the counter and wrote on one of the kitchen cupboards in sure strokes.

You will. You'll beg every time you want to come. You'll get on your knees. Every. Single. Time.

I narrowed my eyes at him. 'Never.'

No matter how much he inflamed my needs, it was just that, a passing buzz. Something to pass the time while I was stuck with him. I didn't want him. Not really. Not if I could be anywhere else. With anyone else.

He was just like Massimo. Mind games and power play. Except nothing like him at all, really.

And you'll enjoy it. You'll come harder than you ever have.

My mouth hung open as he wrote those final words before dropping the pen on the counter and giving me a cocky look.

The absolute fucking big headed twat.

I'd never beg.

Never.

Never.

Never.

TWENTY-FOUR

Phoenix

Why wasn't she giving in? Every signal her body gave screamed of needing my touch, yet still she held back.

I'd have to push my pretty little ember a bit further. Get her to need me as fucking insanely bad as I needed her. My patience for waiting for her to be ready was being tried with every stroke of her skin.

The bedroom light glowed yellow in the inky black of night, Laura's shadow passing the occasional dark shape against it. Using my boot, I kicked a few stones aside before bending down to pick up the flattest one I could find. With a grunt, I flung it out over the calm water, watching it skip four times before disappearing into the depths.

All afternoon I'd avoided the cottage, trying to suppress the need raging through me. Laura had ground her wet shorts against my face and nothing had ever made me feel as feral.

The faint scent of her, the tiny whimpers peppering me from above, the feel of her soft thighs against my cheeks.

Fuck, I'd have spent the day with my face pressed between her thighs had she only relented from her determination to hate me.

The next stone lay cold in my fingers, so cold where Laura had been so warm. Discomfort roiled under my skin, and it only calmed in contact with her. Like a thousand angry ants crawling beneath my skin, only placated in direct contact with our queen.

They screamed at me to go to her. To hold her. To drag sweet please from her perfect pink lips.

I ignored them until I couldn't stand it any longer.

The crunch of my feet on the rocks brought me closer to her. The warmth of the cottage enveloped me the moment I walked in, and I kicked off my boots before grabbing a loop of rope from the tiny, overly stuffed cupboard beneath the stairs.

Laura moved around the bedroom upstairs, her feet padding against the wooden floor above me.

Closing my eyes, I took a slow breath before ascending the stairs.

Laura sang, her sweet voice drifting down toward me, wrapping me in her spell. I kept moving toward her, drawn by an invisible compulsion, a sheer obsession to give her more pleasure than she could stand. To make her want me despite my deformities.

The door flew open, and Laura's song cut off with a gasp.

There were so many things I wished I could say to her. So many words I wanted to whisper into her ears. I hated myself for my limitations. I'd seen enough movies of women crying out with a man tongue deep in her cunt to crave doing it to her.

The sexual limitations had never truly bothered me. I fucked women and paid them well. They didn't look at me, and we completed a transaction. But with Laura? I wanted to make her thighs quiver as I drove her to lose her mind with pleasure.

And I would.

I'd just have to get creative.

Laura sat on the edge of the bed, her fingers digging into the blanket on either side of her soft thighs. She must have seen something in my expression, as when I took a step forward, she rolled herself back on the bed, eluding my grasp.

Her eyes darted to the rope and she made for the door, shoving me hard.

I wanted to laugh.

Oh my fiery one, there's no escape. If I have to trace you across the island and fuck you in the heather, I will.

I caught her around the waist and tugged her toward the bed, throwing her down on the rumpled sheets.

'Phoenix, let me go,' she screeched as I straddled her, pushing her arms up over her head. Like a little hellion, she bucked and writhed, almost unseating me. I wrapped the end of the rope around her wrists, strapping them together, before attaching them to the metal railing of the headboard.

She stopped wriggling momentarily, blowing her hair out of her face.

'So this is it? You've finally had enough and are just going to take what I won't give you?' Laura spat the words at me, but there was an unmistakable glint of excitement between her dark lashes.

Not until you beg.

I spelled out the words slowly against her throat, delight egging me on as she swallowed hard, her throat bobbing against my fingers.

'I'll never beg for you to touch me. I don't want that from you.'

Sliding my fingers around her throat, I tipped her face up roughly and applied pressure as she glared at me.

Her pupils dilated, her lips parting.

She was fooling no one.

My breath heated against my mask.

She's so fucking beautiful.

The soft curves of her chest as she panted between my thighs. Those big doe eyes narrowing at me. The light smattering of freckles across her nose.

Her pulse quickened beneath my fingers and I slid off of her, a laugh bubbling in my throat, trapped there as she tried to kick me.

I grabbed one flailing foot, attaching it to one end of the footboard. She kept struggling until the other foot was similarly detained by my rope, her legs spread wide across the bed.

Fucking delicious.

My rucksack sat neatly between the dresser and the wall, and I fished out a pair of scissors. There were far too many clothes between my girl and I.

Her chest rose as I laid the metallic edge of the scissors against her stomach, snipping through the hem of her shirt.

'What are you doing?' she whispered when I set my hands either side of the cut and tore the shirt from base to collar, the ripping noise echoing through the bedroom.

The need for there to be nothing between her and I flooded me, and I ripped her shorts off while she bucked against the bed.

'Phoenix, stop.'

I paused, taking in her panicked eyes. My girl needed to feel. To give in.

Kneeling between her thighs, I pressed my knee against the crotch of her panties, satisfaction gripping me when she moaned.

Already soaked. My dirty fiery thing.

Grasping her hips in my hands, my fingers sinking deep into her soft flesh, I moved her against my knee. Her mouth made a delicious little O shape.

'I'm not going to ask for it,' she said, despite arching her hips when my hands stopped guiding her against me.

I grazed my fingers over her stomach, her breath hitching. Her face softened as her hips gyrated faster, her panties in disarray.

Picking up the scissors, I cut through the straps and banding of the sports bra she wore, freeing her tits. Fuck, she was beautiful. The pink raised scar on her chest stood out, inciting rage deep inside me. Massimo hurt her. Left his mark on her. I wanted to leave a similar mark right in the middle of his forehead.

I twisted a pert nipple, making her quake against me as she let out a little squeal.

A red flush covered her chest, and she tipped her head back into the pillows, her hands gripping against the ropes restraining them.

I stood.

'No. No! Oh you fucking asshole!' Laura cried, her cunt grinding against nothing but air.

Watching her rage was nearly as delightful as watching her lost in pleasure. Her cheeks practically glowed red as she thrashed on the bed, unable to even press her thighs together with the way I had her tied.

Reaching into my rucksack, still discarded against the wall, I grabbed a black marker pen and popped off the top.

Pinning Laura down to the bed with one hand on her pelvis, I wrote **BEG** in large letters across her stomach.

'No,' she huffed out, her eyes saucer wide at the black marks on her skin.

I hummed to myself, running my fingers along the length of her torso, circling around a nipple. She scowled at me, her brows creasing in the cutest way.

My dick strained against my trousers, every little expression on her face making me harder by the second. What I wanted was to climb on top of her and sink fully into her wet cunt. To have her look up at my face as she fell away from the world in bliss. To feel every single tremor of her pleasure right against my dick.

Holding off physically hurt. But I needed her to want it so badly that she demands I fuck her. To have her know she wants it as badly as I do.

Using the scissors, I snipped off her soaked underwear, holding them up so she could see the evidence of her need.

My dirty girl.

Fuck, I wanted more than ever to be able to talk to her. To taunt her with words all well as my touch.

I had so much I needed to say to her.

Dropping her panties on the bed, I slid my fingers down into the warm, wet welcome between her thighs.

Fucking soaked. All for me. Her mind might not have accepted me yet, but her body had. It craved my touch.

'Oh god,' she groaned when I hooked my fingers inside her.

I'll be your god, if it means you screaming my name out to the universe.

Taking my wet fingers from her, I wiped them over her lips, her tongue darting out to lap at my fingers. Lust laced her eyes before she blinked and turned her face away.

Tsk tsk. Still trying to fight her needs.

Picking up the pen, I wrote across her perfect tits. MINE.

She struggled to read the text, but when she figured it out, she actually growled, much to my amusement.

'I'll never belong to you, no matter how long you keep me on this fucking island.'

Pressing my fingers back inside her soon had her changing her tune to a rich tapestry of moans.

My sweet, angry little thing.

Gripping her chin in my other hand, I forced Laura to look at me, each lusty groan bringing another wave of embarrassment into her reddening cheeks.

If I wasn't careful, I'd get carried away. Seeing her crave me was addictive, like a drug I hadn't realised I'd been missing all my life.

Her stomach quivered with each jerk of my hand and when she opened her mouth, I thrust a thumb inside. Like the perfect little sex fiend, she sucked on it instantly, her eyes fluttering closed.

Within seconds, her pussy fluttered around my other

digits. It actually pained me to remove my hand. Her eyes flew open and she let out a sob.

Tears escaped down into her hair as she thrashed against the bed.

JUST ASK

I spelled out the words against her cheek, my fingers still wet with her saliva.

'Fuck you,' she panted.

OKAY

I pulled my trousers down, kicking them off to the side. Laura's eyes fixed on my dick, it was almost purple at the tip, as desperate for my girl as I.

A groan rumbled in my throat as I threaded my fingers around the head, pumping up and down slowly. She followed every movement. Her eyes on me during the salacious act sent a thrill coursing through me. I'd spent enough years with my dick in my hand, but never for an audience.

She licked her lips when a bead of moisture gathered at my tip. Kneeling next to her head, I stroked the length of my cock right next to her pretty face.

Her mouth opened, and I couldn't resist, leaning forward and smearing my precum over them. Shock crossed her features for a moment, but then her tongue darted out and licked me from her lips.

Yes, my little cock whore. Atta girl.

My balls tightened, my desire for her making me like a fucking virgin again. Sinking into her mouth would be divine. Empty my balls deep in her throat would be a dream.

But I needed her to give in.

Moving down the bed, I knelt between her spread legs, grabbing a pillow and shoving it under her hips to raise them.

Fuck, she was perfect. Laid out for me like my own personal fun fair.

Her clit was swollen; pink, glistening. More than anything, I wanted to taste her. To bury my face there and make her come against my tongue.

Not possible.

Using the tip of my cock, I grazed it against her clit, rapt at the way it made her eyes roll back.

Using my fist, I gripped my cock, running it up the length of her pretty cunt. Her entire body shuddered as it slipped over the entrance.

ASK

I drew the word against her thigh, her eyes dilating at another graze of my cock against her clit.

She shook her head, lifting her hips to try and push my cock into her eager little pussy.

Such a brat. Fuck, when she gave in it was going to be glorious.

I let go of my dick, pressing myself over her, the length of me pressed right between her lips. Arching my back, I slid along her, nudging over her clit then back to her wet heat.

'Holy shit,' she moaned, pulling hard on her bonds as she tried again to slide me into her.

Temptation burned at me. Ate away at my willpower like a hungry fucking beast.

I wanted her so fucking much.

Each time I thrust, my body berated me at the denial of sinking into her.

My breath caught as I ground against her, both of us struggling to battle our own desires to give in. My desire to throw away the need for her admitting she wants me, and her desire to stay steadfast in her denial.

I buried my face against her neck, breathing her in. Her pulse thundered against my cheek, her hips thrusting up to meet my dick with full-bodied desperation.

All I needed was a *please*. A *do it*. Something. *Anything*.

I was going to lose it.

I knelt up, and fucked my fist, making her watch me.

Give in.

Give in.

Fucking give in Laura.

It was too much. Her wet cunt splayed open where I'd thrust between her lips. Her tits rising as she panted against the bed. The rock solid nipples crying out for teeth marks.

Tension gripped me between the legs as I slapped a hand down just above her cunt. My vision blurred and my balls emptied, sending great white ropes of cum splashing against her splayed pussy. Laura watched me lose control, anger filling her eyes as I slowly pumped at my cock, determined not to waste a single drop.

'No,' she whimpered, 'You weren't supposed to come yet.'

I dragged my fingers through the mess, stroking over her clit as she trembled.

Gathering up my cum, I thrust my fingers into her, pushing it deep inside her. It felt dirty. Delicious. Like marking my territory. All mine.

'You can't do that,' she whispered. 'You didn't even fuck me.'

Her body quaked with every thrust of my fingers.

SAY PLEASE

She turned her face away from me, and I laid a sharp slap against her sticky cunt, making her gasp.

My feisty, bratty, slut.

LAST CHANCE

She lay there still on the bed, the fight gone from her. With a sigh, I untied her.

Laura sat up and slapped her hand hard across my masked cheek. Pain blossomed. I'd have taken a million slaps if it meant her skin willingly on mine.

She stood from the bed without another glance at me and stormed from the room. The bathroom lock clicked downstairs and the pitter-patter of the shower drifted up toward me.

She'd been a hairsbreadth from giving in. If I could have contained myself, she could have been in my arms rather than furious.

The bed squeaked as I threw myself back on it, my head thrumming. Tiredness flooded my veins in my post nut state.

TWENTY-FIVE

Laura

Steam billowed in the bathroom around me. My knuckles were white on the edge of the sink, aching from gripping it so tightly.

Warmth dripped down my thighs. Phoenix had pushed his cum up inside me, and I'd wished it was his cock. I had wanted nothing more than him slipping inside me and fucking me hard into the bed.

I hated myself for it.

I hated him for it.

He seemed to know what I craved, and it made me sick to admit I wanted it.

I wanted him.

I wanted him to tie me back down and use me until we were both exhausted.

I craved his fingers and his dick, and I wanted to tell him I'd drink nothing but those god-awful shakes for the next year if he'd just make me come.

With a shaky breath, I pressed my fingers between my legs, gathering his slickness over them. Holding them up to the light above the mirror, they glistened with his pleasure.

Closing my eyes, I pressed them against my lips, my tongue darting out to taste him.

A sob broke free when I opened my eyes and saw myself acting in such a disgusting way.

This wasn't supposed to be my life.

I was supposed to have passionate, sweet sex with a man who came from the same world I did. Not be made to beg a man who stole me for dirty, despicable things.

I climbed into the shower, grabbing a sponge and scrubbed at the pen marking my skin. His words etched into me. I hated them too. Him writing on me had been degrading, yet, had made me hotter than anything any of my college boyfriends had ever done.

Flashes of him above me, his masked face and dark eyes devouring my every noise, the way his thick cock had felt against me, flashed into my mind. With another sob I pushed my fingers against my clit, determined to give myself what he denied.

I couldn't.

It's like he'd disabled something in me, programmed me to his touch. My fingers moved, but the coils of pleasure remained out of reach.

Anger, white and hot flooded me. I picked up the razor from the edge of the bathtub and smashed it into the wall, the metal blade falling free into the soapy water around my feet.

My fingers trembled as I picked it up, holding it next to my wrist. I didn't want to die. But I couldn't deal with

Phoenix driving me to the edge again and again. I felt like I was losing my goddamn mind.

The metal glinted against my skin and temptation clawed at me.

I'd be out.

Free.

And what was there to go back to anyway? Some distant relations who hated my family anyway? Friends who'd console me to my face and gossip about me behind my back? What was the point? Snot leaked from my nose as my tears rivalled the shower for water pressure.

Would Phoenix even care if I did it? Would he send my body home? Would he throw me in the sea like a used piece of rubbish?

I pictured drawing the razor down my arm. Imagined the blood flowing out and filling the tub beneath me.

With a grunt I tossed the blade across the room and sunk down into the tub, water cascading over my head.

I didn't deserve to die.

He did.

Phoenix's chest rose rhythmically on the bed, the visible swath of his face utterly relaxed.

I stood at the doorway, seething in my towel. How dare he just sleep when he's filled me with so much emotion. I'd been in the bathroom trying to decide whether I should end my life, while he had his orgasm and crashed out. Just another fucking pig.

Heat flushed my cheeks the longer I stood staring at him.

Ditching the towel, I pulled on some pyjama shorts and a vest top, half expecting him to wake as I rummaged around the room.

I should just straddle him, take what he's denying me. Who made him the boss?

No. I couldn't. Despite my anger, I wanted to be wanted. For a man to be unable to resist. What kind of fucker can thrust against a woman's pussy but without just shagging her. It was a fucking insult.

My brush sat atop the dresser on Phoenix's side of the bed and I scowled at him as I passed him by. To add insult to injury, my foot tangled in his rucksack, tripping me up. I snagged my knee against the bed and bit down a cry as the sharp pain rang through my limb.

Squeezing my eyes together, I fought the wave of rage that had me wanting to throw the fucking brush through the window.

I levelled a kick into the bag, a jangle greeting me. Time seemed to stop. The jingle sounded an awful lot like keys.

Glancing at Phoenix to ensure he slept, I knelt down and opened the bag. The phoenix clad gas mask sat at the top, worn and smoke stained. It sent a shiver through me, throwing me back to the night he took me.

Placing it on the floor, I raked through the bag until my fingers wrapped around the familiar metal shape of keys. Holding my breath, I extracted them from the bag and gripped them tightly. Adrenaline swooped through me, making my heart thunder as the keychain saying Old Bess glinted in the low lamp light.

The boat keys.

Could I figure out how to make it go? Could I get to someone who could help me?

I had to try.

Staying with Phoenix was confusing me. Making me desire things I had no business wanting.

I looked quietly through the rucksack, hoping to find a phone or some cash, but found neither. Damn it.

What I found were more tools of his trade. Pots with *accelerant* written on the side in faded pen. Matches.

Were they the ones he used to burn my house down? To cover up for the devils crimes against me and my family?

Sweat slicked the back of my neck while my hands trembled, making the keys jingle.

Just go.

I ignored the urging of the little voice inside me, standing and opening the pot of strong smelling goop.

All it took was two minutes, and I'd spread it all around the bed. A moment of guilt clung onto me as I looked at the side of Phoenix's scarred face. He'd escaped the fire once, and lost everything to it's charring embrace.

My fingers slipped against the base of the match as I tore it from the book.

Was I any better than Massimo if I tried to torch Phoenix?

In the mirror on the dresser, I caught the faintest sight of the letters I'd tried to scrub from my skin. The backwards, barely visible BEG on my stomach.

'Fuck you,' I muttered.

The match hissed as I struck it against the textured strip, a flame sprinting into being.

I dropped it on the accelerant smeared bed covers, grabbed the keys, and ran down stairs.

On my way past the kitchen, I stuffed some snacks on the counter into a bag, and picked up the bowl of apples.

With the bedroom window glowing orange, I upended the bowl of apples on the ground as I headed for the boat.

'Sorry, Muffin,' I whispered. 'I'll miss you.'

TWENTY-SIX

Phoenix

The air cloyed in my mouth as I tossed on the bed, reaching out for Laura. A weight seemed to crush my chest with every breath. Turning my head, I willed myself to wake. Heat prickled across my skin, bubbling at the layer of sweat slicking my limbs together.

Fire.

The familiar crackle pulled me to consciousness with an abrupt bump.

I could barely open my eyes with the thick black smoke roiling around me, sinking its obsidian claws into me.

Laura.

Where was she?

Not in bed.

Fuck, I needed to get her out of there.

Angry yellow flames consumed the room, and I thanked the lucky stars that I worked with fire often enough to not be paralysed by the images bombarding my head. May's tears streaking down her smoke stained cheeks as the fire greedily ate its way up her body. My own skin melting and cooking right before me. The wails from both of us that I'd never forget. I grabbed my bag from the floor and pulled my gas mask into place, looking through the licking fire for any sign of my girl.

I fastened my trousers and pulled my bag onto my back, looking around for a way through the raging inferno. My diaries had already curled up into charred remnants.

There was no good way through. Steeling myself, I charged toward the door, hoping my speed would avoid the worst of the heat. My skin didn't sear, but the smell of singed hair followed as I crashed down the stairwell.

Smoke filtered down to the ground floor, but no fire yet.

I cursed my stupid fucking mouth. Every ounce of me wanted to scream Laura's name. To find her. Was she asleep? Was she stuck somewhere, terrified after having been in a burning building before?

The air was too thick to see easily in the cottage, and I stumbled from the sitting room to the bathroom to the kitchen, looking for Laura. Maybe she'd made it out?

Orange descended the stairs, blackening everything in its wake. Goosebumps raised the singed hairs covering my arms. Panic rose in my chest, making me want to wretch. I couldn't stay, but I knew if I went out of the door I couldn't go back in. If Laura wasn't out there, I'd never forgive myself for leaving her.

A glint caught my eye on the bottom step as I made my way past it once again. Something small and round.

It was an opened, emptied tin of accelerant.

Realisation hit me like a motherfucking tank.

Laura had burned down my fucking cottage. *On purpose*. She'd tried to kill me!

Rage engulfed me. Pure, unadulterated anger making my head want to explode.

I made for the door, battling through the thick, black smoke. A brief glimpse of my violin box had me stopping in my tracks. Knowing I shouldn't go back for it, I hesitated. Flames licked greedily at the edge of the box and my stomach leapt into my mouth. I couldn't leave it.

Bracing myself, I fought my way back into the belly of the fire, ignoring the heat grasping at my clothing until the box was in reach. I snatched it up, relief filling me. It had seen me through too much sorrow to meet such an ending. With it firmly gripped in my fingers, I made for the exit.

The cool night air welcomed me like an old friend, kissing me with clean, fresh breaths. My boots sat next to the entrance, where I'd left them, and I shoved them on. I'd need them if I was going to hunt Laura down.

I scanned the horizon, looking for movement. The moon grazed the sea, sending a low light over the rocky shore.

Where the fuck are you?

The stones shifted underfoot as I stalked out in the direction of Old Bess, imagining she would have headed for the boat. I dropped my bag and my violin some twenty metres from my burning home, not needing anything to get in the way of catching my brat.

She'd acted out, and god was she going to pay.

The rocky jetty was silent. I neared my boat, listening out for any signs of Laura. In the distance something cracked in the cottage, sending a burst of flame through a broken window.

Gritting my teeth, I jumped the space between the land and the deck, landing solidly.

Where are you?

Silence met me, even as I made my way toward the cabin. No hurried steps nor quickened breath.

A rush of excitement ran through me, making every one of my senses focus sharply. I'd never felt more like a hunter, seeking my prey. If only I could catch her scent on the wind and use it to track her down.

Darkness filled the cabin, the kitchen as deserted as we'd left it on our arrival to the island. Our previous conversations still marked the walls around the boat in thick black letters. Letter I'd last seen against her sweat slicked skin.

Taking care to soften my steps, I took the slim stairs down toward the bedroom and bathroom area. The air felt undisturbed, but I stalked through every inch of the place, checking cupboards and alcoves, leaving no stone unturned.

What if she hadn't come for the boat? What if I'd got it all wrong and she'd been stuck inside the cottage after all?

The cottage blazed outside, the circular window framing the inferno. The copper and gold dancing along the waves reflected the destruction burning on shore.

My stomach dropped. *I had to go back.* To make sure. What if I'd left a jar of accelerant there somehow?

I took the stairs back up toward the deck, when the

unmistakable jingle of keys sounded. Freezing in the stairwell, I listened intently.

There it was again, the light crash of metal on tiny metal.

The little wench was trying to steal my fucking boat.

I would have laughed if I could. Damn, she had some balls.

With stealthy steps, I picked my way toward the control room, my view diminished slightly by my gas mask. I considered taking it off, but opted against it, wanting to remind her of that first night we met. The night I'd pulled her from a burning building, only for her to leave me in one.

No, that night would be a night she *never* forgot.

Laura had her back to me, her little pyjama shorts tucked into her pretty, round backside as she struggled to find which key fit into the control panel.

Even after her trying to kill me, I wanted her. I wanted to possess her every fucking breath.

'Thank god,' she muttered as the key slotted into the hole.

Too late, I thought.

She let out an ear splitting scream as I dragged a finger over her shoulder, turning wide eyed. Her scream stopped short at the sight of me in my smoke blackened clothing, peering straight back at her through the eyeholes of my mask.

When I tipped my head to the side slightly, fear filled her beautiful face.

Good.

We stood, staring at one another, each waiting to see what the other would do. She cracked first. My keys crashed against my mask as she launched them at my face. Instinct made me flinch to the side, and she took the moment to barrel past me, shoving me aside.

My little ember had no idea how much chasing her was riling me up. I turned to run after her, my cock already tenting my trousers. She'd find out soon enough.

Her hair whipped around her like a silken cloud when we hit the deck. I cut off her way to the jetty, my pulse leaping at her panicked look.

I didn't expect her to launch herself over the edge and into the sea.

It didn't stop me from throwing myself in after her.

The water met me with its chilled embrace, stealing the air from my lungs for a minute. Wiping the water from my mask, I looked around me. Splashing sounded to my right side, and there she was up ahead, wading toward the shore.

While my face might not have moved, I grinned internally.

The water pulled at my clothes, tugging me to and fro. It's grip lessened the shallower it got, until I was chasing Laura through the shallows.

Close. So close.

Her hair stuck to her back, her wet clothes sticking to her soft body making me feral. I gained on her with every waterlogged step.

She made the mistake of glancing back at me, stumbling over a submerged rock and landing on her hands and knees in the water.

Satisfaction hit me the moment my fingers sunk into her wet hair, pulling her up and forcing her backwards over a large, black rock. Her feet kicked against the water, her back arching against the stone beneath her.

'I'm sorry,' she spluttered, tears streaking her cheeks.

It wasn't her apologies I required. It was her desperate pleas and her thighs gripped around my waist I sought like a starved man. Punishing her for burning my home was tempting, but I knew that more than anything I wanted her desire in place of any retaliation.

She flailed, repeating her sorry sobs as I tore her wet clothing from her body, revealing her to the stars.

I'd driven her too close to the edge too many times. I'd rattled her mind. It was time to rectify that.

Wrenching her thighs apart and setting my knee between them, I thrust two fingers deep into her cunt. The warmth contrasted with the icy water sloshing against my legs and it was like a homecoming. A shudder made her body quake against the rock, the fight instantly leaving her. Curling my fingers up against the inside wall of her pussy brought a whimper of need tumbling from her lips.

That's it, my little obsession, give it all to me.

Reaching over her, I wrapped my other hand around her neck, squeezing the sides tightly. There was no doubt I'd make her come all over my fingers, but she'd feel my ire at burning my cottage with every fucking stroke.

Her breath stuttered as I thrust deeper, her wetness coating my fingers.

Words burned in my throat, so many things having to go unsaid. Her hips raised from the rock as I forced a third finger into her. Her thighs gripped against my leg, nails scraping against the rock on either side of her.

'Phoenix,' she moaned, her pleas a salacious croak. 'Please... don't stop.'

I twisted my wrist, her body convulsing in reaction. A

wave sent a spray up over us, the cold water making Laura's nipples peak. Her whole chest was covered in goosebumps, right from the bullet scar down to her spread thighs. The light from the burning cottage reflected in every water-drop along her soft skin. I wanted to devour every salty droplet.

The moment her eyes rolled back, and her thighs crushed around me, I slowed the strokes of my fingers inside her. Our eyes met and I dragged my other hand from her throat, writing *beg* over her chest.

'Please make me come, Phoenix. Fuck me, touch me. Whatever you want. I'll do anything.'

I slid a fourth finger inside her, stretching her pink cunt wide. It was enough to send her tipping over the edge.

Her cries of pleasure filled the night sky. They touched everything around us from the sea to the stars. She came hard and fast with my name a sordid prayer on her lips, her inner walls crushing my fingers with need.

And that first, desire-fuelled, cry filled the hole inside my chest that had long been empty.

That's it, my sweet obsession, come for me like a good fucking girl.

TWENTY-SEVEN

Laura

Nothing mattered.

Nothing except for Phoenix and those glorious fucking fingers of his. My hips were raised fully off of the rock, Phoenix's other hand sliding back up to my neck to pin me down as wave after wave of pleasure coiled through me.

The rock grazed my fingertips, the sensations between my thighs becoming overwhelming when Phoenix didn't let up after my orgasm subsided.

'Phoenix,' I whimpered. He relaxed my hips back down toward the rock, his thumb coming up to stroke lazily against my clit. Each circle made my body shudder, making me want to scoot back from his touch. The hand around my neck slid down to my pelvis, pinning me to the black rock.

GOOD GIRL

He used his thumb to spell out the words on my clit, and with each letter he dragged another pathetic moan from me.

I shouldn't enjoy him calling me that. But I did. Pleasure bloomed again, building with each of his touches.

The gas mask covered most of his face, just the deep, dark eyes visible behind it. My own face reflected back at me in the glass when he tilted his head. Wet hair stuck to my shoulders from jumping into the sea, my own splayed pussy reflected when he glanced downward.

The sight was salacious, his fingers moving down to pump rhythmically in and out of me.

'Fuck me,' I groaned, desperate for more now that he'd broken the seal. It was like all the pent up need he'd stoked in me bubbled to the surface, an unquenchable fountain of lust. 'Please?'

The hand around my throat fell away as I pushed myself upright, leaning forward and undoing his trousers. His scarred fingers caressed the side of my face, tipping my chin upwards. A shake of his head told me I didn't have to... but I wanted to.

I'd burnt his cottage, and instead of hurting me, he'd pleasured me and called me a good girl. After everything, he truly did want me. His rage would have overridden his arousal otherwise.

Speaking of arousal...

The head of his dick popped free from his trousers, thick and hard between my fingers. His skin silken to the touch, but veined along the rigid length.

Licking my lips, I wondered how the hell it would all fit in my mouth.

Phoenix's fingers traced my lower lip, tugging it gently downwards.

'Can I taste you?' I asked.

Phoenix gripped his dick and leaned forward, the sea sloshing around us. He dragged the tip over my lips before pulling it away when I tried to lick it. My brows furrowed and I narrowed my eyes, glancing up at his masked face.

Then he pressed the head against my lips, slipping between them. I moaned and his eyelids fluttered behind the glass.

Swirling my tongue around the head, he tasted like the sea, faintly salty and smokey. Another reminder of the cottage burning to our left.

I pressed my fingers against his hips, using the leverage to move forward and backward, working him with my mouth until he slipped his hands into my hair and began to fuck my face.

Tears pricked at the edges of my eyes, his cock slipping further into my mouth with each thrust. I swallowed him down, wanting to give him the pleasure he'd finally given me. A deep, guttural noise came from his throat, and it made me even wetter than I had been.

My hatred for him had fled, leaving nothing but fiery heat. Maybe I'd finally lost the plot. Maybe. It was some sort of response to protect myself.

Well, fuck it. Whatever it was, I was done fighting it.

With a sudden jerk, Phoenix pulled my head backwards, a string of saliva attaching us together. I swallowed, waiting to see what he'd do. Lust glazed my vision for a handful of heartbeats. I waited to see what he'd do.

His grip tightened in my hair, almost painfully so. Within a moment, he'd pushed me onto my back, spreading me wide with his other hand. I could scarcely breathe with need, it was like my blood was boiling on the inside, leaving me nothing but a mess.

The tip of his cock rubbed against my swollen clit, and I wrapped my legs around his hips trying to pull him into me faster.

PATIENCE

His finger-whispers only fuelled my desperation.

'I've got no more patience, Phoenix, so FUCK ME,' I demanded.

He entered me in one sharp thrust, my whole world tilting on its axis. Using the hand in my hair, he kept my eyes on his, through the mask, as he let me adjust to the fullness.

'I wish you could talk to me,' I whispered, arching against the rock to take in a little bit more of his glorious dick.

The way he rolled his hips stole any further words, dragging a low moan from me. I dug my fingers into his arms, gripping tightly as he began to thrust into me, fucking me back into the rock with harsh, desperate thrusts. Every scrape digging into my skin only stoked the pleasure. My toes curled, and I wrapped my arms around his neck, breathing him in with each ragged pant.

He felt *right*.

The way the heat of his body engulfed me. The way we fit together so perfectly.

Flutters stormed my insides, sweat gathering where our bodies met.

SAY MY NAME

His fingers had dropped to the back of my neck as he spelled out his impassioned plea.

'Phoenix,' I whispered against his neck, wishing I could drag his mask from his face.

His thrusts quickened, forcing little cries from me with every scoop of his hips. It was all too much. He ached between my thighs, stretching me with every vicious slam of his pelvis. Our breath harried, his groans stuck deep in his throat while mine filled the air. The heat from his body against the icy chill of the sea. Even the passion with which he fucked me, I could palpably feel it thrumming in the air. Never before had I felt so utterly desired as I did at that moment, accepting his pleasure.

COME FOR ME

The jerky strokes of his finger on my neck were my undoing. I let go of the part of the old me I'd been desperately holding onto and sank into an orgasm that shook my entire world.

The rhythmic clamping of my muscles had him quaking against me, my moans lost to the night while he filled me with ropes of hot cum. My orgasm knew no bounds, slamming through me and stealing away my free will, leaving me utterly defenceless to the onslaught of desire he hailed down upon me.

Stars exploded.

Worlds ended.

Pandora's box was ripped wide by his cock deep inside.

As I trembled against him, his cum seeping out with his slowing strokes, tears fell.

I knew I'd beg him to take me again, and again.

He'd played my body like his violin, and now I was trapped by the beautiful song he'd wrapped around us. A song borne of gasps and moans, of desperation and desire.

Phoenix had bewitched me.

A sob tore from me as the weeks of betrayal and loneliness

came to a surface. The loss of my family hit me full force with the emotional wave the orgasms had unleashed.

Phoenix picked me up, cradling me against his chest. A wicked shiver wracked me as the moments of passion depleted, my naked and soaked form catching up to reality. He walked us close to the cottage, before stripping himself off, ditching the gas mask even, his scarred face on full display.

The rock he sat on was warm beneath us, and I burrowed against his chest, his burning home warming us.

I cried for my loss.

I cried for my weakness.

I cried for the cottage.

I cried for him.

All the while he held me. Giving me safety and warmth I didn't deserve.

I cried about that, too.

TWENTY-EIGHT

Phoenix

Blackened ash clung to my fingers as we picked through the cottage's carcass. Little remained untouched by fire or smoke.

Although I had lived there for as many years as I'd spent at home with my family, the cottage had never felt like it was mine.

It was my uncle's. A place of loneliness and anger. If the walls could speak, they'd have whispered about black eyes and my beaten body. They'd have spoken of so many nights spent sobbing. They'd have screamed about the boy who vanquished the evil plaguing him, only to be wrapped in more years of solitude.

But they would speak of Laura too. Of her warmth filling the barren rooms, her kindness attracting the local animals. Of her stealing that pathetic boy's heart.

My eyes found her through the jutting wood and blackened stones, looking forlornly at what was once one of my diaries. Even after a night sobbing on the beach, marked by the stone I'd fucked her against, my cum drying on her thighs, she was the most exquisite woman I'd ever seen.

Fucking her had been better than I'd dreamt it could be. So different from the clinical liaisons I'd had in the past. Her eyes had brimmed with desire, even with my scarred face showing past my gas mask. There was no recoiling from my touch, she'd wanted more. No, needed more.

My addiction to her touch had been unleashed, every metre between us feeling like a tortuous chasm.

Abandoning my search for anything surviving, I moved toward the one thing that truly mattered.

'I'm so sorry,' she whispered, looking at the devastation at her feet. 'I don't know what I was thinking. I was just... so mad. At you. At me. I snapped.'

The charred paper of the diary crumbled in her hands, and I'd have been lying if I said there wasn't a tug at my chest. It was all I had left of Mum, Dad and May. My childhood ramblings.

Lifting a hand, I took the book from her hands, and dropped it to the floor. Returning it to the old part of me it belonged with.

The previous night had been a crossroads. One of those life altering moments where you can go in a host of different directions, changing your world forever. I chose the road Laura stood at, ready to follow her into whatever future lay ahead.

Mine.

Now I'd had her in my arms, throwing my name to the universe in screams of pleasure, I knew there was no going back for me.

No matter what. She was mine.

I took her hand gently, leading her carefully from the destroyed building to where Muffin awaited, happily munching the discarded apples he'd found on the ground.

'Is it time to say goodbye?' Laura asked, running her fingers over the pony's mane, her eyes shining in the afternoon light.

I nodded.

'Will we come back?' The pony nuzzled into her as she spoke.

I nodded again.

With the cottage gone, I could start fresh. Have a home built worthy of a woman like Laura. Somewhere with the finest things so she'd want to stay. Hell, I'd even build the bloody pony a stable and grow it a whole orchard of fucking apples if it meant she'd be content.

Plus, the trees would be great for tying her to while I filled her up time and again, until her womb was bursting with me.

The thought of having her carry a child for me, to bring us both a family clawed its way into my mind. Of getting her off of her birth control and stuffing her full of bucket loads of my cum until it took hold of her. Of doting on her while she grew round with a baby that was half me, and half her.

I was hard at the thought. She'd glow, alright. And they'd be mine. Mine to protect. Mine to cherish. Never would I be lonely again.

My touch made her bite her lip as I traced a finger down her spine. We'd only had the few clothes in the boat left to wear, other than our wet things. So she wore a pair of my shorts and an old T-shirt, but even in that, I wanted nothing more than to press my face into her skin and inhale her.

'I'll miss you,' she said to the pony, burying her face into his mane. 'Be good and look after the place until we get back. I'm leaving you in charge.'

The pony had no idea what she was saying, but gladly appreciated the scratches anyway. A lump of jealousy flared in my throat. Would she be so sad to say goodbye to me? Or even after our night of passion, would she leap at the chance to be free of me? Would I ever truly know?

I didn't care to find out.

The boat came to a stop as I turned off the engine, idling it. We were about halfway to the mainland, on our way to replenish supplies. Stretching out my aching muscles, I made for the deck, where I found Laura laying on one of the low wooden benches, the lowering sun dancing off of her legs.

I'd taken to carrying a marker pen with me, ready to answer her by writing on whatever surface was available. Walls, the deck, furniture, hell even our skin. Whatever was available was fair play. Taking it from my pocket, I lifted her feet and sat beside her, resting her legs over my knee.

'Hey,' she said, her smile like a thousand watt light. I was the moth ensnared by her presence.

HI

As much as I loved touching her, I was growing weary of never being able to say exactly what I wanted too. Anything longer than a few words was too much for the finger spelling, it took too long. The writing helped, but even then our conversations were stilted, full of long pauses while she awaited my words. I wanted to talk to her. To ask her questions and answer hers.

I wanted to be able to pull her against me and whisper dirty little things into her ear. To lick and suck at her skin. To kiss her. I'd never been kissed.

'You okay?' she asked, sitting up and looking into my uncovered face. I still felt naked without my lower face mask on, but I'd left it in my bag, wanting to get used to being around her without it. I wasn't immune to the fact that sometimes her eyes drifted to my scarred mouth and held there a moment too long. Sitting in my discomfort was a new battle for me to fight.

I nodded at her, placing the pen down on the bench. It promptly rolled off and along the deck. Laura let out a giggle. I rolled my eyes.

'Will you play for me?'

The violin case had been unsalvageable, but my violin and bow had survived the fire, a little smoke stained, but usable. It was the first time she'd asked me to play. When I'd taught myself, I either did so on the other side of the island, or would get told to shut the fuck up by my uncle.

Having her request a performance made me both as pleased as punch, and as shy as a school kid asked to perform in assembly. Laura had heard me play, but never had I done so to please her.

Running my hand down over her leg, I nodded.

'Thank you. There's something enthralling about your music backed by the waves. It makes me feel like a mermaid caught in a fairytale.'

I fetched the instrument, playing a few practice notes and getting it tuned back up. Butterflies filled my stomach as Laura sat before me, her head resting on her knees, looking utterly engrossed in my every move.

The song I chose was an old one, one I'd found written by hand on lined paper, all of the notes, but no words. I didn't even know its name. It had fallen out of a sheet music book I'd picked up at a charity shop once in the West Isles.

The notes sang out, filling the space around us with life. Music sprang from my violin, wrapping us both in its cascading notes. I closed my eyes to the world, letting the music pull me into its grasp. My fingers danced along the strings, playing having been one of the activities that had kept them dexterous despite the scars.

I missed a handful of notes when her fingers grazed the hem of my trousers. Caught up in the music, I hadn't noticed her approach.

'Keep playing,' she whispered.

The wind cooled where her warm touch blazed. She freed my cock, and took it into her mouth, coaxing it until it filled to bursting at her bidding.

She hummed along as she sucked, sending throaty vibrations along my shaft. I wanted to drop the violin and take her in my arms. To be inside her, pressed against her. But I obeyed her plea to keep playing, the tempo increasing along with the eager strokes of her mouth.

My heart thumped in my chest, a heavy drumming to accompany our music.

She knelt before me, her big eyes watching me play. Her mouth turned up at the edges, despite being impaled by my dick, every single time I faltered.

She was playing a game with me, and as the minutes passed, she started to win. My concentration faltered with every deep groan she gave. Saliva dripped from her mouth whenever she pulled back to breath. Pink swollen lips wrapping around my dick was a heady sight, and it was my undoing.

With my bow still in my hand, I pushed my fingers into her hair, pressing her firmly down over my cock as my balls tightened. Her eyes widened, her nostrils flaring when I forced my dick down into her throat, fucking at the tight ring marking its entrance.

Her moans turned to splutters, but I held her fast until my balls emptied into her, shooting ropes of hot cum down into her waiting throat. My breath was rapid as I held her there for a few moments longer, giving her every single fucking drop and waiting until she'd swallowed it down like a good girl.

At last, I pulled her away from my cock, her breath coming in sharp bursts. Kneeling there, lips swollen and tainted with cum and spit, I'd never wanted to kiss her more.

TWENTY-NINE

Laura

Three days of shake drinking had me desperate when we pulled up to the harbour.

Phoenix opened the safe hidden in one of the kitchen cupboards, pulling out a phone and some cash.

'Can I come with you?' I asked, wanting to feel solid ground beneath my feet again. 'Please?'

Phoenix's brow knitted, his gaze darting to the bustling harbour.

You'll leave, he wrote on the counter top.

'I won't, I promise.' I couldn't say the thought hadn't crossed my mind. Telling someone I still existed, that I'd been shot and taken from my home. But to what purpose? To go back? For Massimo to know I'm alive? The courts would never convict him. I'd be dead before it ever got to that point, likely a corrupt police officer would take me out on his behalf.

Men like Massimo never lose.

Phoenix stared at me intensely, the marker tapping against his thigh.

'I promise I'll stay with you. I don't want to be alone.' His chest inflated then deflated with a sigh and I knew I'd won.

I threw myself at him, pulling him into an excited hug. It took me a moment to realise we hadn't exactly hugged like that, and I stood awkwardly with my arms looped around his muscle clad back.

My heart jumped when he reacted, wrapping his arms around me and squeezing me tight. I had no idea how long it had been since someone hugged Phoenix, but he hugged me like he'd never been embraced before.

Emotion flooded me as he sniffed above my head, holding me to his chest. One hand cupped the back of my neck, tracing something in the midst of my hair.

I couldn't make out what it said,

'I can't understand,' I mumbled against his chest.

He moved back a touch, tipping my head upward and I swear I could see the smile glittering in his eyes however impassive his scarred mouth remained.

'Go freshen up,' he wrote on the counter, squeezing the words into a gap. Day by day there was less space to write, his side of the conversation spreading over every surface.

'Why? Do I smell?' I grinned as I said it.

He swatted my ass on the way past me before writing YES above the doorway.

'You'll pay for that,' I laughed. Phoenix waggled his eyebrows at me before ducking out of the cabin door.

Being back in civilisation felt utterly alien. People chatted about their weekly shop. Children begged parents for some e-number filled goodies with pouty faces. An old couple inched down an aisle at a glacial pace, supporting one another by the arm.

Life bubbled around us, yet Phoenix looked the most uncomfortable I'd ever seen him. Bar grabbing some spare t-shirts, underpants and socks, he'd barely glanced at the shelves. Guilt ate at me as I picked up a pack of profiteroles, practically salivating. I placed it back on the shelf, not wanting to indulge when all Phoenix had was his stupid strawberry shakes.

Pushing the trolley forward, I moved to the dairy shelves. When I picked out a bottle of milk and placed it in the trolley, I saw the profiteroles placed on top of the eggs. I glanced back at Phoenix.

He touched the back of my arm, his fingers quickly drawing words against my skin.

Treat yourself.

A smile stole over my face.

'Alright freak?' A voice said to my left.

Phoenix's eyes narrowed, fixing on the young teens who stood across from us. While he'd worn his mask to the shop, his scars were still visible above and below the phoenix emblazoned fabric.

His fingers dropped from my arm, tensing into a fist beside his thigh.

'Oh my god, he's so gross,' a girl said, laughing and nudging her friend.

I turned to face Phoenix, sliding my hand into his and applying light pressure to his fingers.

'Ignore them,' I said, forcing his eyes to mine. 'They're just stupid kids. They don't define you. Your scars don't define you.'

He took a deep inhale through his nose, his eyes flicking back to the idiots.

'Ew, are you, like, into him?' One of the girls directed her words at me.

It wasn't something Phoenix and I had discussed, not even when our limbs had been entangled with me screaming his name into the sheets.

'He's more man than any of you little fuckers will ever be or be with.'

The kids looked stunned at my cussing, and I desperately wanted to laugh at them. The arrogance of youth never failed to astound. But had I been any better when I first saw his scars? I may not have spoken out, but I'd been just as shocked.

The kids threw us a dirty look before moving on down the aisle.

I didn't drop Phoenix's hand. Not even when we awkwardly moved our groceries onto the conveyor belt, nor when he counted the cash to pay.

It was silly. And wonderful.

THIRTY

Phoenix

Relief swamped me the minute we were back aboard Old Bess with Laura singing softly in the kitchen as she put away the groceries.

I took to the deck, readying for sailing back out to sea a bit, maybe settling in one of the natural havens around the coast a bit. Away from people.

Realistically I knew decking a teenager was a bad idea, but the rage had wound me up all the same. Until Laura had slipped her fingers into mine.

In all my years, I'd never thought a pretty girl would willingly hold my hand. Sure they'd take my cash and bury their face in a pillow. With their eyes closed I felt like every other customer. My lovely little ember had reached out and healed a missing part of me. She'd held my hand in public. Not just for a moment to stay my anger, but for the remainder of the shopping trip. She'd weathered the stares and whispers with a sunny smile that melted away my ire. If she could take it, so could I.

A light rain smattered the deck, and I shoved my mask into my pocket to fully feel the sprinkles against my face.

The boat swayed gently with the incoming tide, and gulls squeaked over the harbour, swooping down over the distant cafe along the stony harbour side.

For the first time since the night I threw Laura into my arms, I turned on my phone.

Multiple beeps came through from various numbers, all likely to be burners. No one kept a number long in my game.

Two potential jobs, now long past. I didn't need the money, but had some shitty texts when I'd failed to help them. Unreasonable pricks could maybe just stop killing each other for a few weeks.

There wasn't a lot else. It's not like I had family or friends wondering where I was.

Another beep rang out.

> Where the fuck is she?

Oh shit. The coroners must finally have figured out Laura wasn't amongst the charred corpses in the burnt mansion. That the old man I'd killed didn't pass for a young woman on further inspection.

Ignoring him was an option. But no response would likely make him more suspicious.

Damn it.

> Who?

> Laura. The seemingly undead bitch from your last job for me.

My fingers whitened around my phone. I tried to infuse my veins with calm, I needed to feign ignorance. If he knew I had Laura, he'd kill us both. Or he'd try, at least.

> I just torched the place. No idea what you're talking about.

The three little dots danced on and off repeatedly. *Please buy it.*

> Listen to me, you dumb fucking animal. The police are looking for her, which means they are looking at me. If I find you've got her I'll make you sit and watch while every single one of my men takes his turn with her. When they've fucked her to death, they'll start on you. Last chance to let me know anything you know. If I find you lying, I'll track you down and make you wish you'd never been fucking born. So I'll ask you this once. WHERE IS MY FUCKING BITCH?

My jaw clenched. My possessive side rearing up like a cornered animal.

I sent one final text, before turning the phone off, smashing it beneath my boot, and kicking it into the ocean.

> She was never yours.

No one knows who I am. He can't find her.

I tried to assure myself the whole time I steered the boat away from shore. I needed distance until I could think it through.

I didn't know much about Massimo, except he was ruthless. An awful lot of truly terrible people shuddered at the mention of his name.

Eventually we pulled up in a sheltered bay, one long forgotten but once used by Scottish bootleggers and other unsavoury sorts.

My sort.

Laura joined me, looking delicious in a short pink floral dress and an oversized white cardigan. She must have showered and preened, her lips looking extra juicy with a bright coating of shining rose.

She carried a tray in her hand, and twirled carefully as she neared me.

'Do you like it?' She asked.

I nodded. Frustration whipped through me. Laura deserved more than nods. She deserved a man who could tell her she was the most beautiful woman in the world. That I'd give my right fucking arm just for one of her smiles.

She sat beside me on the bench, her skirt barely reaching her thighs.

God damn.

Every inch of their soft, smooth surface needed to be worshipped.

The tray held my usual smoothie, but also two bowls of delicious smelling spicy soup.

Laura's cheeks pinked as she picked up her bowl and spoon. 'You don't have to eat it if you don't want to. I know you're used to the shakes and...'

I didn't need another word. She'd cooked for me. We could share a meal that wasn't artificial tasting smoothies. No one had cooked for me since my parents died, my uncle never transitioning me from the high calorie shakes. Soup would never have been able to nourish me to the same level, so I'd never bothered with it. What was the point?

Now I had a point. My pretty little flame.

I turned my head as I pushed the straw into the smooth bowl.

'It's okay,' she said. 'There's no need to hide for me.'

I closed my eyes and took a steadying breath, before tasting the soup through the small hole on the side of my mouth. It slid quickly up the straw, warm, spicy flavour hitting my tongue.

I groaned, the sound caught as ever in my throat. Fuck. I'd forgotten what flavour was. I'd had nothing but cold, powdery fake strawberry for over a decade, and the soup may as well have been Michelin-fucking-starred.

'You like it?' Laura asked, her face breaking into an absolute beaming smile when I eagerly nodded. 'It's carrot and potato curry soup. I don't know many recipes by heart, but I know that one. We had to make it in school during home economics.'

Was there no part of my life she couldn't make better. Well, except burning down my house.

I finished my soup in record time, revelling at the heat

inside my stomach. The soup was like a warm hug from the inside out.

The sun dipped near the horizon while Laura ate, sending an array of colours dancing across the clouds. Laura caught my gaze over the sea, placing her bowl down and scooting a little closer to me. Wrapping my arms around her, I pulled her back against my chest, leaving my fingers resting against her shoulder.

Thank you, I spelled out in slow strokes.

'You're welcome.'

Her chest rose against my arms, a contented sigh falling from her lips as we watched the dark shape of a bird murmuration swooping against the brightly coloured sky. It never failed to amaze me how they did so, moving as if one.

We sat there until the night conquered the day, a chill settling over us with each passing moment. Our conversation came in fits and starts, my finger spelling proving too cumbersome for anything more. Frustration filled me up, making my skin crawl.

I didn't want a stupid fucking pen. Or to have her read my broken words against her skin.

'Phoenix?' she asked. I'd been so lost in my thoughts, I hadn't heard what she'd said.

Sorry, I spelled out, *Lost in thought.*

Laura turned to face me, her thigh pressing up against my leg.

'I asked if you'd ever been kissed?'

Shame heated my cheeks at her question. Of course I'd never been kissed. I was a scarred monster. Most women couldn't even make eye contact, far less kiss me.

Running a hand through my hair, I shook my head.

'Can I kiss you?' Laura bit at her lower lip after asking, those big doe eyes focused on my face as she awaited my answer.

It was all wrong. I should be the one trying to kiss her. Making her feel wanted.

After a moment's hesitation, I gave in, nodding once.

I reached out, cupping her face in my hand as my pulse hit a new speed record. Dipping down to meet her, her lips put pressure over my would-be mouth. There wasn't a lot of sensation in the old tissue, but it still sent electric shock through my system. Her breath was warm against my face, still smelling of spice. Leaning up, she peppered my face with a series of tiny kisses. My tongue pressed against the back of my teeth, desperate to be free from its cage to taste my girl.

Enough was enough.

My reflection glared back at me in the mirror. The sun had just come up, glinting through the porthole and dancing on my blade.

The tissue covering my mouth was a knotted web of scars. Thicker in some spots, and thinner in others. Grazing my tongue along the inside of what my lips would have been told a similar story. Sealed in all but that one small spot.

Like tree roots, the scars spread up the side of my face, and down over my neck. The memory of feeling my flesh bubbling was still there, my cheek pressed against burning metal as I tried to grasp May's fingers, her terrible screams making me stay there despite the smell of burning fat and skin.

I'd worn the scars so long I couldn't picture the face that had existed before them. No matter what, I'd never be handsome. No matter the mornings I spent punishing myself with body weight exercises to give myself a physique intimidating to others. No matter what I wore, not how expensive my cologne was. The first thing everyone saw was my mangled face.

Except Laura. She'd seen past it. She'd pressed her lips against the ugly skin, and smiled up at me like I'd given her the best kiss of her life.

Lifting my blade, I pressed the tip through the gap, avoiding hitting my tongue. The knife was wickedly sharp, more akin to a scalpel than anything else.

Ten shaky inhales later, I still hadn't mustered the courage to do it. The blade trembled as I applied a little pressure at the corner of my mouth, a singular drop of blood escaping. The tiny cut made me wince.

Withdrawing the knife, I leant against the sink, watching the thin rivulet of blood drip down my chin and land on my bare chest.

A wave of dizziness hit as I gripped the handle of my blade, my hands growing clammy. My pulse thundered.

Come on you useless prick.

One quick cut and you can have Laura against your tongue.

The metal glinted in the light as I raised it to my mouth, opening my jaw wider to stretch the scarred skin. My breath caught as I panted through my nose. Steadying myself, I dragged the edge through the scarred tissue, fighting the scream that I wanted to wail. The skin was tough, and I had to wrestle the blade through it, blood splattering down into the sink. My chest painted red as I neared the other side of my mouth, tears streaming down my cheeks. I inhaled deep.

Through my mouth.

My teeth were coated in bright red blood, but I could SEE them. I ran my tongue along their scarlet covered surfaces, tasting the coppery liquid. Pain radiated, but so did excitement.

A laugh broke free. It was the most ridiculous sound I've ever heard, but despite the ache thrumming around my mouth I couldn't break the smile.

THIRTY-ONE

Laura

The sound of the bedroom door clicking woke me. I rolled over, expecting Phoenix to be beside me, but found the bed empty.

Sitting up, I glanced to my left. I shrieked when Phoenix filled the door, his torso dripping in red.

He moved forward climbing onto the bed and coming toward me, his face breaking into a grin.

'Oh my god! Phoenix!'

Pressing bloodied fingers to my cheek, he tipped my face up to his. His mouth opened, his torn lips leaking afresh as he did.

'Laura,' his voice was a croak, stiff and broken.

Beautiful. His one word was music to my ears.

'Phoenix,' I whispered, hardly believing what he'd done. Jagged, torn flesh bleeding with every movement of his mouth. Lifting my fingers, I deftly placed them against his chin, scared the touch would hurt him.

'Why did you do it like this?' I asked.

His eyes darkened, fingers scooping my chin and pulling my mouth closer to his.

'I couldn't... wait another... minute without knowing... what you taste like.'

Heat filled me at the urgency in his words, at the sheer desperation within them.

Our mouths met in coppery embrace, his tongue tentatively seeking mine. It should have disgusted me, but I opened my mouth wider, tasting him, drowning myself in his desire.

I hadn't realised how much I'd been holding back. How much I craved kissing. Whimpering, he slid his mouth down my throat, his teeth grazing against my pulse. I fell back into the pillows, giggling as he pushed my nightshirt up, sinking his teeth into one of my nipples. The giggle turned into a yelp, until he soothed the pain with the flat of his tongue.

A deep groan vibrated against my nipple, and it sped through me, hitting me right between the thighs.

'Oh my god,' I moaned, threading my fingers into his hair. He left a stream of red wherever he touched, a visible marker of him on my skin.

Hot breath caressed my wet pussy as he moved between my legs, spreading me wide.

'Laura, you have no idea the depth of my obsession with you.' Phoenix's voice was deep, the cracked resonance tinged with a Scot's accent. I hadn't even considered he'd be Scottish, despite spiriting us away to an island way up north. It was a voice I could listen to forever. 'I have craved feeling you against my tongue since the moment we met. I have inhaled your scent but been denied your taste for too long. You are going to be my first feast. The taste I've longed for more than any fucking food on God's green earth.'

'Please?' I whimpered, his breath taunting me with every word.

A rich chuckle sounded against my clit, and I could have sworn I'd died and gone to heaven.

'I love it when you plead,' he said, his tongue grazing against the spot right above where I needed him.

'I need you.' I pushed my fingers further into his hair, trying to press his mouth down on me. Blood dripped from his newly fashioned lips, reddening my cunt.

It was dirty, and yet, made me so fucking horny I was practically humping his face in desperation.

'My perfect, needy little slut. Open and ready for me.'

Fuck me. If he'd driven me to the point of burning down his house without a mouth, he was going to kill me with one.

The first tentative stroke of his tongue made my world spin on its axis. The growl of need he gave disjointed me from reality entirely.

Clinging onto his hair, I whimpered, not sure if the way he slid against me was from his blood or my wetness.

'Fucking delicious,' he grumbled against me, his breath hitching.

Tenderness fled. He pressed his mouth against me, not caring about any pain he felt. Lashing with his tongue, sucking me into his hot, wet mouth, sliding two fingers inside me and roughly fingering me. There was no sweetness. Lust fuelled us both.

My hips crashed upward, meeting every wild stroke of his tongue. He ate like a ravenous beast, devouring my cunt with a fervour that only stoked my desire further.

Moans and whimpers filled the cabin, growls and curses following.

'I could live right here,' he moaned, sliding a third finger inside me.

I lost any semblance of control I may have had. Blood coated and panting, he tipped me over the edge. I came hard against his face, wetness flooding us both. My chest was so tight I worried it might explode as I clenched my thighs and rode his tongue, desperately seeking out every last drop of the pleasure he inflicted upon me.

My limbs turned to jelly, flopping on the bed as I sought to gain my breath.

Phoenix had other plans.

He didn't stop. Wrapping his arms around my hips, he held me tight, sucking my clit back into his mouth.

It was torturous having already orgasmed.

'I can't,' I whispered, gripping fistfuls of blanket. 'It's too much.'

'You will,' he moaned, face stuffed between my still quaking thighs.

'Phoenix,' I breathed, trying to wriggle free.

There was no escaping the onslaught of his tongue. Sensation overwhelmed me and I fought to overcome it. But I had little choice. Phoenix was a man possessed.

'You are going to spend the entire morning as my breakfast. I'm going to make you squirt on my tongue again and again until neither of us can take any more.' His voice was gruff and commanding, making my stomach fill with butterflies.

'I don't think I can take any more,' I said, a whorl of pleasure already peaking.

He pushed a fourth finger inside me before grinning up at me with his slash mouthed smile. 'You'll take a whole lifetime of it, my little ember.'

His nickname for me fell over me as he pried another orgasm from my sweat and blood caked body. I screamed, tugging at the bedsheets while he doubled down with his tongue against my clit. My vision blurred and my breath ceased as the pleasure peaked, another gush of hot liquid flooding the bed around us.

'Phoenix,' I cried, my whole body quaking uncontrollably.

That rugged laugh met me, right against my soaked pussy.

'Saying my name like that only fuels me, baby. Now, come for me again, my fiery one. Soak us both in your need.'

Within minutes, he had me back at the precipice, both begging for more, and crying with overwhelm.

Soon the orgasms rolled into one long rollercoaster, draining my body until I was nothing but a limp, useless form on the bed. Only then did he climb into bed, spooning me as I spaced out.

His hard dick filled me, and I sobbed from how swollen my pussy had become, from the height of the emotions he'd wrung from me.

'Sweet Laura,' he crooned as he thrust tenderly inside me. 'My perfect cumwhore. You want me to fill you up don't you?'

Through tears I stuttered. 'Yes.'

'You are mine,' he growled against my neck, his hips crushing into my ass as he inhaled me fully. 'And I'm going to make sure I never leave you unsatisfied. I'll fill you until you fucking burst.'

My head swam, his words both thrilling and soothing. Never had I felt a man so obsessed with me. Me?! My imperfect body drove him to this level of compulsion. How?

'And one day, I'm going to fill you with so much cum, you'll grow round with my children. I'll make you my wife, then breed you. We'll grow a perfect little family.'

The words made me hot. They shouldn't have. I wasn't an animal to be bred upon his whim. But the idea of him fucking his babies into me made a dirty coil of pleasure curl inside.

'Not yet,' I murmured, turning my head to meet his torn lips, not caring when they smeared mine with a fresh layer of scarlet.

'No, not yet. I'm going to be selfish with you first. Spend years with you all to myself. Finding out every way I can make you see stars with my tongue, my fingers and my cock. You'll scream a thousand orgasms to the stars before I breed you, but when I do, you'll spread those thighs and take it like a good girl, won't you?'

Fucking hell.

I couldn't even answer, because with a violent scoop of his hips, he was filling me with hot streams of cum, and I fell right over the edge with him again, my pussy convulsing so hard it stopped him even being able to thrust.

He was right.

I was all his.

THIRTY-TWO

Phoenix

Laura's face was a picture of concentration as she threaded the needle through the scrappy skin. I fought the grimace brought on by the painful tugging.

'You should have gone to a hospital,' she admonished, those big eyes fixing on me. I couldn't talk without disturbing her mending, so I let her tell me off. Not caring as long as she was still pressed up against me, her legs in my lap while she stitched me up.

'I'm not exactly someone who excels in needlepoint.'

With gentle touches, she cradled my face as she worked. Mint mingled on her breath where we'd cleaned up after our messy morning.

It was all worth it.

Worth the pain. Worth the blood. Worth the fear.

Making her come against my tongue had been the pinnacle of anything I'd ever known. Power had surged through me at the demented sounds my mouth had wrangled from her pleasure engulfed body. I was completely, and utterly, addicted.

I'd been so unsure on whether the words would come, whether my vocal cords would even still work. The years of humming along with my music must have kept them in working order. Communicating my thoughts with Laura, without the delays or the difficulties, had been thrilling. So much so, it pained me to have to sit still while she sewed my torn skin into some sort of lips.

The softness of her thighs was the perfect distraction from the odd sensation of the medical string pulling through my would-be lips. Grazing my fingers over them, working my way ever higher, watching as her pupils dilated.

'Behave,' she murmured.

'Never,' I said, letting my thumb glide over the crotch of her shorts.

She snipped off the end of the string, finally finishing her task. The fact she'd sat me down and looked after me left me feeling warm and fuzzy. Not since my initial hospital stay had I had someone caring about me.

Passing me a washcloth she'd had steeped in warm water, she instructed me to wash away the fresh blood the needle had drawn.

'It's not perfect,' she said, her voice breathy.

'I don't care.' I leaned forward and kissed her softly, not wanting to burst the stitches. Admittedly, I'd happily burst them if it meant pouring myself into kissing Laura, but I had a feeling she'd be less than amused.

Some ten minutes later, we sat on one of the wooden benches, watching the seals poking their heads out of the water below us. Laura had cut up various fruits, cheeses and meats into tiny cubes, and for the first time in years, I actually had textured food.

It was a lot to handle at first.

Slowly, I tried a few pieces, enjoying the sweet burst of the fruit against my tongue. Fuck, had grapes always been so damn tasty?

'My mum always had high expectations for me, I guess. I just didn't live up to them. Not smart enough. Not skinny enough. Not pretty enough. It's why Massimo made me fall so hard so fast. I never believed a guy like him would ever want to marry a woman like me.' Laura and I had been discussing our pasts as we ate, and it was a good job her mother was already dead. I'd have been tempted to find her and do it myself if she hadn't been.

'She was crazy. You're perfect.'

Laura looked down at the strawberry piece between her fingers. 'I'm not.'

'I don't just say that as a loser with no mouth. I mean it. The moment I laid eyes on you I was a goner. And then you came at me with all the blaze of a fire and you had me obsessed.'

'You're not a loser. Mouth or otherwise. It just took me a while to see past how we met. Stealing women isn't exactly an honourable pastime.' She grinned before popping the strawberry into her mouth.

'Not women. Just you.'

I pushed the plate of food aside and pulled Laura into my lap, trailing my fingers up and down her spine.

'So what now?' She asked.

'More sex?' I lifted a brow.

'No, you rampant fiend. You need to let your mouth heal

for a bit. I mean what's next? Do we just stay on the boat forever?'

Bar filling her with my babies, I hadn't seriously thought about what came next. Especially with Massimo now looking for her.

'We'll rebuild the cottage, no, build a better one, with whatever you need. I'll build you a stable for that pony of yours, and enough bedrooms to spend years filling them with a family.'

She blinked up at me. 'You want to make a family with me? I thought you were just dirty talking.'

'One day. After I've had you to myself for a good while. My family is nothing but a distant and painful memory, and yours were shit. We deserve a real family. With all the eye-rolling stuff other families do. Board games, long walks, stupid Christmas jumpers. I want it all.' It was something I thought would always be out of my reach.

'Whoa, one thing at a time,' she laughed, 'I've only just come around to the idea that I'm staying willingly.'

'I'm going to marry you, Laura. I want to worship you every single day for the rest of my life.'

Her face softened and she wrapped her arms around my neck, pulling me tight.

'Okay, but you'll need a better proposal than that.'

'Noted,' I said, inhaling the fruity scent of shampoo lingering in her hair.

THIRTY-THREE

Laura

People still stared at Phoenix in the street. Instead of hiding, he smiled his scarred smile and held his head up high. Pride flourished in me as I watched him.

He'd come so far from the angry child in his diaries.

It had been two weeks since he'd cut open his mouth, and happiness bubbled inside me. The thick muscles of his left arm bulged under the weight of the shopping bags, while his other hand held mine. I trailed him, dawdling at the shop windows.

We'd lasted as long as we could in our lust-filled haven, but with the two of us eating, our supplies had soon diminished and we braved a village shop.

A light rain smattered us as we walked, but it couldn't steal the smile from my face. I'd spent so many years wishing to be free of my family's expectations, and despite the trauma and heartbreak, I'd found myself there. Phoenix spent every day making me feel seen. Adored. Desired. The way we had met had been the biggest of red flags, but after all was said and done, he'd saved me. From the fire, from the bullet, and from my depressing future.

'Come on, slow coach,' Phoenix said, smiling over his shoulder at me.

'You could drop my hand and I could take some of those bags.' His one arm looked ready to burst, thick veins coating the rippling muscle.

'Not a chance.'

A familiar face flashed on the TV mounted inside the newsagents. I froze, terror gripping me in its vice. My blood ran cold as Massimo filled the screen.

Phoenix stopped, turning to see what held my attention.

Subtitles danced along the bottom of the screen.

'I'm appealing for information on the whereabouts of my fiancée. She was taken from her home by a known associate of criminals, who killed her family and set fire to the building.'

His words reached through the screen and wrapped around my lungs, squeezing them until I couldn't breath.

'Darling, Laura, if you see this, know that I am looking for you. That I will find you and bring you home.' Massimo touched a perfectly folded tissue to the corner of his eye, making a great show of his mock grief. 'I still love you.'

Phoenix was by me in a second, pulling me into his arms as my pulse seemed to stutter to a stop.

'He knows,' I whispered.

'It's okay. He won't find you,' Phoenix's voice quavered, but he held me firmly in his arms, not caring as the rain picked up and soaked us both. Placing the shopping bags on the ground, he took both hands and cupped my face, turning it up toward his. Tears mingled with rain on my cheeks. Massimo tried to kill me. If he found me, he'd succeed.

'We're in a village. People will see us.'

'And we'll get back to the boat and disappear. We have enough food here to last us a few weeks. I can arrange for more to be delivered directly to the island and we'll pick it up there. I know some guys who owe me a favour or two.' When I glanced back at the TV screen through the window, he pulled my attention back to him. 'Laura, I will protect you. I promise.'

'Every day I'm going to be searching the horizon, fearing the day he comes for me. Massimo isn't the kind of guy who gives up.' My teeth began to chatter as the rain soaked us through.

'Neither am I,' Phoenix said with a growl. 'And I'll lay his goddamned head at your feet before I let him touch a single hair on your head.'

I wanted to believe him.

THIRTY-FOUR

Phoenix

Fucking Massimo.
 The man was going to die. Painfully.

Laura sat on the bed, her arms wrapped around her legs and staring out at the sea. The wind was picking up a touch, and I'd dropped the anchor for the night, hoping to get through the dark haze diminishing my girl's light.

I moved in beside her, wrapping her up in my arms and watching the waves with her.

'I was getting so excited every time we spoke about the future,' she said, her voice too soft. It broke a little piece inside me to see her hurting. 'But I just can't now. I can't get the picture of him on the TV out of my head.'

'You're safe here,' I spoke the words with confidence, hoping they'd soothe her.

'I feel sick every time I think about it. When I close my eyes I see him there, the gun pointed at me, my family's blood splattered over his expensive suit. His eyes. God they were filled with so much hate.' Laura trembled in my arms, her breathing growing more rapid with each word.

'It's okay,' I said into her hair, kissing the back of her neck softly. 'I've got you, Laura, and I won't let him hurt you.'

I only hoped it was true. Massimo used his power to corrupt far and wide. I'd been one small part of his extensive chain of terror. There were many others who'd sell their right bollock for the chance to give him information he needed.

'No one even knows my birth name. They've never seen my face. The boat is still registered under my uncle's business partner, and they're both dead.'

Laura turned in my arms, her brow quirking. 'Will you tell me your name?'

I hesitated for a moment. 'I buried it a long time ago. My uncle just called me boy, or something far less kind. When I started burning for pay, I assumed the name Phoenix.'

'You don't have to,' she assured me, her fingers moving up to slide into the back of my hair.

But I wanted her to know every part of me. Even the parts I'd long hidden from the world.

'It's Thomas.' I stumbled over the name, it felt alien on my lips after so long. 'Thomas James Porter.'

'Thomas,' Laura repeated, the name sounding far more pleasant from her.

'My dad used to call me TJ,' I said, a blurry version of his face sifting through my mind. Not for the first time, I wished I had a picture of us all together. A reminder of the boy I'd once been, and the people who I'd called my family.

'My dad used to call me pudding. And not in a sweet way.' Laura shrugged and then laughed. 'God, they sucked.'

'They really did,' I agreed, pushing a strand of hair away from her face with my thumb.

'Do you want me to call you Thomas?'

'No. It's a name that died when they did.'

'Good, I like Phoenix much better. My man who rose from the flames.' Laura's eyes fell back on the roiling water outside. 'Phoenix, I need you to make me forget about Massimo for a while. I need a break from the worry.'

'What can I do for you?'

'Fuck him out of my head.'

I knew what she needed. More than a quick romp in the bed, or a fuck in the shower. Laura was asking for an escape. To be pushed to a place where she'd be so lost in sensation that she wouldn't even remember her name.

Stoking the fire-bins on deck, I had them roaring, sending an orange wash over everything on deck. The wind was picking up, waves crashing against the stern, salt water splattering against my shoes.

I pulled Laura up onto the deck, her eyes covered in a makeshift blindfold. She shivered as the wind hit her naked skin, instantly pebbling those perfect nipples.

The boat rocked and she fell heavily against me.

'Phoenix,' she breathed, her voice trembling.

'Trust me,' I crooned, running a hand over her round ass.

I'd spent many a stormy night on the deck, feeling the power of nature. Nothing made me feel more insignificant in the face of an issue. What were our problems in the face of the power of the sea?

Guiding her toward the railings, right to the point where they stretched out over the sea, I used a reel of rope to fasten her wrists behind her, stretched to the rails to the left and right. The metal rail cut into the soft flesh of her stomach, her tits suspended over the wild sea below.

I pressed against her, pulling her hair tight in my fist and tipping her head to the side.

'Tonight, you're going to feel fear and lust combine. I'm going to push you until there's nothing left in your head but me. Do you understand?'

'Yes,' she moaned, already melting beneath my touch.

'I'm going to use all but that pretty mouth tonight, and only because I thrive on hearing you squeal for me. I want fucking Poseidon to know I'm cumming deep inside your hot little ass.'

'My ass?' I watched as she bit her lower lip.

'No. It's my ass now, Laura, and I'm going to christen it. You'll take it like a good girl and be rewarded for it.'

'Yes,' she whimpered, her body quivering.

Leaving her blindfold on for now, I slid one hand between her thighs. There was no doubt she was already hot and heavy. Her wet cunt welcomed me, swallowing up my fingers.

'There's my girl, so fucking eager, aren't you?'

She nodded, her head lolling back against my shoulder. I pinched at her clit and grinned as her whole body shuddered.

I rolled letters against her clit, too quickly for her to know that they spelled out my feelings. *I love you. I love you. I love you.*

Words I hadn't dared dream about for a lifetime. Words I'd never appreciated the last time they were said to me. Words that almost choked me every time I spoke to her.

Her breathy pants soon turned to wickedly wanton moans, her hips gyrating against my hand.

'That's it, Laura, come for me.'

I waited until her body shook, her hands pulling against the bonds which held her fast, to whip off her blindfold.

Her scream could have woken the fucking dead. A wave crashed into the boat right as her orgasm intensified, splashing icy water over us both. She coughed, and spluttered in my arms, and I didn't move until her pussy relaxed its hold on my fingers.

'Phoenix, untie me! This is crazy.'

'Do you trust me?' I asked her, taking my wet fingers and bringing them to her mouth.

'Yes...'

'Good, then you'll behave. Now lick your cunt from my fingers like the perfect little slut you are for me.'

Her eyes hooded at the light degradation, her mouth opening without any further hesitation.

'Taste how wet you are. How your pretty little cunt reacts to my touch.'

Her moans made me feral. Need gripped me as her tongue wrapped around my scarred fingers, licking at them like a pet.

'Such a very good girl.'

I moved to the side, placing my lower face mask over my chin. Her eyes blazed as she watched me, her lips opening.

'For old times' sake. You think I didn't see how turned on my masks made you? I could smell the desperation from between your legs. Now hold on tight, I'm going to fuck your sweet cunt without letting you come. Because the next time you do it'll be with my dick deep in your ass.'

'And if I don't beg?' She asked, her big doe eyes fixed on me.

'You will.'

THIRTY-FIVE

Laura

Heat from the burning metal bins warmed my back, while the icy sea splashed up and froze my front. The contrast had my head spinning.

Phoenix positioned the head of his big dick against my entrance. My legs shook in anticipation as he waited there, teasing me with infuriating nudges.

'Phoenix,' I groaned. 'Fuck me already.'

'Such a needy little cock whore. So impatient to be filled.' His dirty words made my cheeks heat, but it only made me try harder to wriggle back onto him.

Fingers threaded into the back of my wet hair, pulling my head back and making my tits stick out over the rough sea below. The reminder of it had me feeling queasy. The storm was picking up and another large spray of sea water hit me right in the face. I gasped a breath, unable to shake the water from my face with the way Phoenix held my hair tight.

'I'm obsessed with this body,' Phoenix crooned, his deep

voice sending butterflies right down between my thighs. 'Every inch. When I'm not with you, I count down the moments until you're back in my arms.'

I writhed my hips, succeeding to pop the very tip of him inside me. The moan shuddering out of me was utterly shameful. I'd never needed a man as badly as I needed Phoenix. He tapped into me in a way no one ever had. Left me craving his next hit of passion.

With an impassioned grunt, Phoenix slammed into me, stealing my breath and making my body shudder. I panted, adjusting to the sudden feeling of fullness, his cock stretching me wide.

'Was that what you wanted? To be stuffed full of dick?' His words were lightly mocking, and a sweet mix of shame and desire filled me.

'Yes,' I moaned, shifting my hips to feel him shift inside me. 'Please, I need more.'

'Oh, Laura. I'm going to fuck you like I hate you. Use this divine body in the way it was designed to be used. But know I don't hate you at all…'

Gripping tight onto my hair with one hand, and my hip with the other, he pulled back and smashed back into me, making me cry out over the waves. The railing I was tied to ground into my stomach, winding me. The sensations hit me all at once, pain crashing with pleasure, making me squeeze my thighs together, trying to apply friction to my clit. That only made the squeeze around his dick tighter.

'I'm going to fuck every last worry out of your pretty little head until there's nothing but pleading and desperation left in there. Until you can't think of a single thing but my fucking dick impaling you.' Phoenix's rough words had me grinding back against him, meeting his harsh thrusts.

His breath was hot on my neck, coming in sharp bursts as he fucked me ruthlessly. Losing control, his teeth dug into the back of my neck through his mask, pain radiating as he bit me.

The feral action had my knees quaking. He wrapped his arm around my waist, holding me up as he drove his cock into me with abandon. His hips smacked into me so hard, my feet suspended off the deck with every heavy thrust.

I was lost to everything but him. Like a rag doll being toyed with by its master. He played my body as expertly as his violin, bending me to his needs.

I loved it.

I *needed* it.

My pants grew heavier, my eyes rolling, even the splashing of the waves against my chest didn't take away from the mind blowing pleasure building between my thighs.

When he pulled away, dropping my feet to the deck, I let out a pitiful cry.

'No... Phoenix! Don't stop.'

'You know what I want.' His words were inky, his fingers grazing over my well fucked pussy.

I shivered. I'd never been fucked in the ass. But I wanted to come. Very, very badly.

'Will you be gentle with me?' I asked.

'No. You'd be disappointed if I was. I'm going to *claim* this ass. Mark it as *mine*. Watch as my cum drips from it.'

Imagining his cum dripping out of my ass made my thighs clench. I wanted it. I wanted him to own every part of me.

He leaned in close, his mouth grazing my neck, his mask gone. 'I've never fucked anyone in the ass either. You'll be my first.'

Despite the rolling boat, he dropped to his knees behind me, his arms wrapping my hips and his mouth sinking over my clit.

It was like lightning striking right between my legs. Sensation washed over me with every divine stroke of his tongue. He went at me with gusto, not holding back as he devoured my cunt.

I was at the edge within a minute, my arms straining against the ropes which held them fixed.

His tongue lashing stopped and I cursed him out viciously.

'You know what I want,' he said, his voice dripping with wickedness.

'I want you to fuck my ass,' I panted, I'd have given him anything just to have him take me over the edge again. 'Please?'

His mouth settled over my cunt again, licking and sucking until my brain melted to mush. Then it moved higher, his tongue darting between my ass cheeks. I squirmed in his hands, my mouth gaping as his tongue pressed into the tight ring. I bucked against the alien feeling, squeezing my ass at the invasion. Phoenix was relentless, sliding one hand around to my pussy and slowly fingering me until I relaxed my ass again. The sensation of his tongue went from alien to immeasurably pleasurable as the minutes passed, until I found myself pressing back against his face, needing more.

'Look at you, Laura, grinding your ass against my tongue. You want my big dick splitting you apart, don't you.'

I did. Fuck, yes I did.

'Phoenix, if you don't fuck me, I think I might die.'

He chuckled heartily before moving away from me.

'Phoenix,' I called, turning my head to see where he was. 'If you leave me here, so help me, I'll cut off your balls.'

'Don't worry my pretty pet,' he said as he came back into view holding a bottle of olive oil. 'Just making it easier for your tight fucking ass to take all of me.'

He drizzled two fingers, holding them up so I could see the pale green liquid glossing them.

Apprehension filled me as he pressed them against my ass, rubbing in circles.

With his other hand, he tilted my face, grasping my cheeks between his fingers and kissing me roughly. With his kiss distracting me, his fingers worked slowly into my ass. He swallowed down my needy moans, until his fingers finally slipped past the ring of muscle and into the forbidden spot beyond.

'Fuck,' I whisper moaned into his mouth.

'Soon, my pet.'

He held me there, his fingers working my ass until I began to relax, pressing back with each stroke, my tongue lashing his with need.

'See, I know what you need. Your body calls to me, Laura.'

'Yes,' I muttered, my eyes closed, lost in the new sensations. The pleasure coiling in my stomach felt different, tighter and more intense. My thighs started to tremble, and his laugh surrounded my mouth.

'You're not coming until I'm inside your ass, my little firecracker.'

'Then fuck me before I cry.' My body was as taught as a violin string from his teasing. I needed to let go.

'I'll fuck you while you cry, your tears will only make me come all the harder.'

At last, he stood. I listened intently, over the crashing waves and howling wind. Cold shuddered my body without his heat against me. Looking down, another wave of fear hit me at the churning sea below.

The wet slop of him fucking his oil covered fist filled the air, and I moaned when he spread more oil over my ass.

Then pressure made me cry out as he pressed the head of his dick against the tight bud of my ass.

'Don't fight it. You're going to get ass fucked either way. Fighting only makes it more painful for you.' Phoenix's voice was harsh, his own desire peaking along with mine.

I tried to relax, my eyes widening when he inched forward. The stretch was unbearable. I let out a needy sob, my legs shaking at the intensity.

'I can't...' I whimpered.

'You are,' he assured me, his cock sliding into the tight ring, pain searing.

I choked on a sob, tears dancing down my cheeks.

'Mine,' he growled, gripping my hips hard and pulling me back onto him.

I came before he was even fully inside me. A harsh, unforgiving orgasm ripped through my body, leaving me ragged as he slid the rest of the way inside me. My ass vibrated around him, wave after wave of overwhelming pleasure tearing into me.

'There's a good girl. Coming all over my cock. Your

perfect ass milking my dick. There's more baby, more for you.' Desire hitched his every word. 'Fuck, you feel so fucking good, Laura.'

My mind was sludge. Useless and filled with nothing but pure bliss. My body was his to bend to his pleasure, all control of mine vanquished. He slid out to the tip, before pressing fully back into me, until his hips squished against my well oiled ass.

Each heady stroke extended my orgasm, making my body shudder around him.

The sounds falling from my lips were animal-like. Truly, I sounded like his pet.

'It's too good,' he groaned, every deep sound coming from him only making me hotter. 'I'm going to come.'

'Fill me,' I begged, wanting him to mark my last hole as his.

Phoenix wrapped both of his hands around my neck, pulling me harshly against him as he fucked my ass with abandon, the intense stretch making me sob. Despite my cries, my body reacted to his deep thrusts by tensing around him, a final, muscle quaking orgasm making me scream out into the storming night.

Phoenix tensed, his hands tightening around my throat, stealing my breath as he unloaded deep inside me, filling me to bursting with his hot cum.

'I love you,' he stuttered, his hands dropping to my chest and stomach, his panting breath against my shoulder. 'More than I ever thought I could love anyone.'

His sweet words were the end of me. I broke completely, tears falling, great heaving sobs wracking my body.

I wanted to reply, to tell him I loved him too, but I couldn't.

He'd truly fucked me into oblivion.

THIRTY-SIX

Phoenix

I tucked Laura into the bed, wrapping the duvet round her and sliding beside her. She'd barely spoken since our intense session, so I'd carried her into the cabin, cleaned us up and soothed her.

She shivered beneath the duvet, my arms covering her as I petted her hair, waiting for sleep to claim her.

I'd told her I loved her.

I tried not to let the fact she hadn't said it back grate on me. Giving into the attraction had come much later for her than I, it didn't mean she wouldn't get there. Plus, she'd been in no fit state to say anything after we'd fucked.

Silken strands of hair slipped between my fingers, her breathing settling as she warmed back up. Soon, her breathing settled into a slow, rhythmic beat, and I wallowed in my self pity for just a little longer.

I could only hope she'd get to where I was. Because I was all in for her.

Soaking up her sweet presence, I let my mind wander to the place I'd been trying so hard to distract her from.

Massimo.

Despite being as off the radar as I could, I knew his poisonous claws ran deep in Scotland. If he set his heart on it, he wouldn't settle until we were both dead.

Laura's cheeks flushed, her eyelashes fluttering against them as she sank into a deeper sleep.

Grabbing a hoodie and jogging pants, I headed for the kitchen, making myself a strong cup of coffee. Taking a sip, I screwed up my nose and promptly spat the horrible liquid into the sink.

Urgh. Why were people so obsessed with *that?*

I swilled my mouth out with water and topped up a glass.

With the storm picking up, we were anchored for the night, but sleep felt a million miles from my head. The intense play should have left me ready to crash alongside my girl, but all the worries I'd stolen from Laura only seemed to compound mine.

Pulling up the boat's computer, I logged into the roaming Wi-Fi. The VPN I used should dissuade anything from tracing back to me.

Using the digital access I had to my phone number, I made a brief log in to the web version of the number.

A series of messages pinged up. A few jobs. A few cancellations of the offers, either because it was too late, or more worryingly because they'd heard Massimo was looking for me and didn't want to hire a dead man walking.

There were no messages from Massimo. He wasn't the sort to rant down a text message like an angry teenager.

Logan McGowan's name popped up with a handful of unread messages.

I clicked through, wondering if he needed another job done for his family, it had been the job I'd just completed before diverting to Laura's house.

> Hey, I'm not sure if anyone's reached out. Massimo is out for your blood. Something about you stealing his fiancée? He's issued a reward for you both, dead or alive. I've attached the pictures he's sent out. There are bounty hunters clamouring to be the first to cash in. Look after yourself man. If there's anything I can do, let me know.

There were attachments in a few separate messages, and I opened each one.

Laura and I in the last little village we stocked up in. Pictures of us through a shop window, my scarred beast-like face next to her sweet face. Who had taken them?

I punched the back of the built in sofa bench, cursing as pain ricocheted up my arm.

Why couldn't the universe just let me be happy? All I wanted was to start building a life that would please Laura. That would have her being by my side forever.

And now that fucker Massimo intended to at best rip us apart, at worst kill us.

The hairs on the back of my neck stood up, my anger roiling like the sea beneath me.

Massimo would burn. Him and everything he held dear.

If it was the last thing I did.

THIRTY-SEVEN

Laura

Massimo stood in front of me, his gun held to forehead. My heart beat erratically as I tried to look around for a way out.

'You were supposed to die, Laura. Instead you're shacking up with a freak. You're disgusting.'

'But he loves me...' I protested.

Sweat dripped down my face. Why was it so hot?

The flames. I hadn't noticed the flames.

'Massimo, we need to get out of here,' I coughed.

The gun clicked, followed by his hollow laugh as I squealed.

'Don't worry, we'll find which chamber has the bullet soon. This time I won't miss.'

Couldn't he feel the heat? My eyes stung. I needed to get out.

'Laura?' Phoenix's voice was soft, somewhere deep in the burning edges of the room.

'Help me!' I cried out. Massimo turned and let off a handful of shots into the flame.

'No! Stop it.' I lunged for his gun, but I was too slow. I watched as a bullet tore from the barrel, heading straight for my face. There was nothing I could do, I was frozen to the spot awaiting the pain.

Hands wrestled my shoulders.

'Laura... Wake up.' Phoenix's voice was more insistent this time. Closer.

Sheets tangled around me as I roused, the dream dissipating. Phoenix came into hazy focus, my eyes groggy.

'Phoenix?' I mumbled.

Pulling me up to sitting, he helped to untangle me from the sheet. I cooled down almost instantly, a fresh breeze coming through the open door and wrapping around me.

'You were dreaming,' he said, concern furrowing his brow. 'The same nightmare again?'

I nodded, reaching for the glass of water by the bed and taking a long drink.

It had been two weeks since we'd seen the TV appeal through the shop window, and instead of my worry decreasing over time, it had been compounding. By day I could mostly push it to the back of my mind, but by nightfall Massimo stalked me through my dreams, turning each into a familiar nightmare.

'I don't think we can stop for food,' I said, my heart pounding at the thought.

'We have too. Even with the stock of shakes I have here, we're running low. Most of my stash was in the cottage. We need to stock up.'

As if mocking me, my stomach let out a deep grumble.

Phoenix leaned forward and grazed his healing mouth over mine. 'We'll be quick, in and out. You can stay on the boat, I can go alone. Your picture is far more recognisable than the blurry one of me.'

Panic seized me, and I pulled his fingers into my hand. 'No. You can't leave me.'

'It's safest on the boat.'

'It's safest with you,' I said, my voice cracking at the idea of being left alone near the port.

Phoenix tugged a hand through his hair before scooping me up and pulling me against his chest. 'Then we'll stay together. We can get you a hat and shades, something to disguise you a little. I've ordered the food for pick up, we just need to get to shore and make a quick trip to grab it.'

'Okay,' I breathed, apprehension still making me feel sick.

'I'll make you a cup of tea and a piece of toast before we pull into the dock. Rake through my drawers there and see if you can wear something that'll disguise you a bit.' Phoenix injected calm into his voice, deliberately slowing it. But beneath the calm, it rang out the same worry I felt.

Every movement I made was drenched in foreboding, shadowed by some sort of black dog waiting to pull me back to Massimo. The ever lingering fear of my dreams dogging me by day now, too.

Splashing water on my face at the sink, I tried to shake the feeling of impending doom, but no matter what it remained. In the circles beneath my eyes. In the prickling sensation at the back of my neck. In the dullness of my eyes.

I threw up a silent prayer to God, or the universe, or anyone who was listening. *Let us get the food and get back to the boat safely. Please?*

THIRTY-EIGHT

Phoenix

I breathed a sigh of relief as Old Bess came back into view, our footsteps quick on the old stone harbour side.

We'd stocked up on plenty of food, both of us weighed down with the stuffed bags. The water containers should have been topped up while we were away too. All set to hit the seas.

'Almost there,' I said, encouraging Laura who still looked as pale as a sheet. She'd barely spoken a word since we pulled into the town.

Anger bubbled up in my stomach, with every fearful glance she gave. Massimo had become a monster who haunted her dreams, the one place I couldn't protect her. An insidious vampire leeching away our chance at happiness.

It was no good, I wouldn't spend our lives fleeing and hiding. Massimo was on borrowed time. I'd find a way to get to him, and indulge myself in seeing him pay for hurting my girl.

I climbed the ladder up onto the deck one handed, my other arm straining with the weight of the bags. Plopping them down on the deck, I reached over to take Laura's bags before offering her a hand onto the boat.

Her face visibly relaxed the moment she set foot aboard. Wrapping my arms around her, I pulled her to me for a quick kiss, my body still filling with wonder at the graze of her tongue against mine.

'I can put the shopping away while you get us back out on the water,' she said, her brow creasing as she glanced back to shore.

'By nightfall we'll be back at the island, docked next to the shore. Muffin will be delighted to see you.'

A smile lifted her lips, erasing the worry line on her forehead. I'd burn the whole damn world to keep that smile on her beautiful face.

After lifting the bags into the kitchen area for her, I headed back out onto deck to ready Old Bess for the trip.

I hummed to myself out of habit while I worked, scanning the dark clouds gathering over the horizon.

My stomach lurched when A blood-curdling scream came from the cabin. I dropped the rope I had in my hands and ran toward the door, panic scorching me.

All hell broke loose in the kitchen, two dark, hooded figures attacked Laura, who slashed at them with a large kitchen knife. She was backed into a corner and there was no doubt they'd overwhelm her in seconds.

Wrestling a fire extinguisher from the wall beside the kitchen, I picked it up, slamming it against one of the intruders' temples. He fell down like a sack of shit, but I wasn't quick enough.

The other held Laura with the knife to her throat, his arm wrapped around her to hold her still.

We both froze, her eyes wild and filled with terror, my heart thundering as I looked for a way to get to her.

'I don't need her alive,' the man said, his accent thick and rough. 'Take one step and I'll slice right through her neck.'

Fuck.

A thousand thoughts dashed against my mind, too much risk. I had to hold onto the thought that while Massimo would want me dead, he'd probably prefer Laura alive.

The man at my feet was out of it, still against the floor.

I dropped the extinguisher and held up my hands. The man I'd knocked out had a gun. And it was pretty close to my right foot. Grabbing it wasn't an option, the moment I moved, the knife wielding guy would stab Laura.

'Alright, I surrender,' I said, keeping my hands above my head. I stepped back against the wall, pressing my foot down on top of the dropped gun and sliding it backwards.

'Mickey?' The guy said, trying to peer around the kitchen cabinets without losing his hold on Laura. 'You okay?'

Mickey didn't answer.

The man moved with Laura, keeping the knife digging into her neck.

Shit, if he came too close he'd see the gun beneath my boot. Laura's eyes met mine and I flicked them quickly to the floor and back up. Her brow wrinkled in confusion. The man was close enough to see his friend, but hadn't rounded the kitchen counter yet. When he used his toe to nudge his co-intruder, I mouthed, *distract him,* to Laura.

'Oh my god,' she cried out, turning in her captor's grip

and threading her arms around his waist. 'I thought no one would ever come to save me!'

She burst into the most pitiful tears, and the man froze, looking unsure on what to make of this new development, the knife still pressed against the side of Laura's neck.

'He took me! I've been waiting for someone to come rescue me. Did the police send you?' She sobbed against the hooded face.

The moment he glanced at her, I used my foot to slide the gun up the wall and into my hand, not waiting for a moment before aiming and blowing a shot through the fuckers brain.

A red rain splattered Laura, who let out a scream as the body fell away from her, the knife clattering against the floor.

'You could have shot me,' she gasped.

I shrugged, moving over beside the man with half a skull. 'I'd never hurt you. Well, only when you beg for it.'

'Oh my god,' she murmured, 'I think he got brains on me. What will we do with the other one?'

'Help me get him tied to the chair. When he comes back round we'll see what information we can get out of him before sending them both down as chum.' I hauled the unconscious man upright and pulled him toward a seat.

'Massimo knows where we are, doesn't he?' Laura said, her voice small and tight. 'He's not going to stop sending them.'

'He'll stop,' I said, pulling tightly on the ropes I bound the unconscious man with. A puddle of blood pooled beneath his friend, spreading over my floor. I couldn't even throw him over the edge until we'd got well out to sea.

'How do you know?'

'Because I'm going to kill him.'

THIRTY-NINE

Laura

Rain smattered the man's face, making rivers which fled down into the collar of his top.

I shivered, the cold wind freezing against my wet clothes.

Silently, he watched as Phoenix finished securing the weighted containers to the dead man's body.

I could hear my heart beat through the noisy wind as Phoenix rolled the man to the side of the boat, sliding the weighted containers over the edge, the ropes attached pulling the wrapped body overboard.

Then he was gone. One splash, and out of our lives.

Our captive dug his nails into the material of his trousers, his wrists reddening against the ropes holding him. Seeing the way Phoenix disposed of his friend without a care, had him finally looking nervous.

Phoenix joined us, wiping his hands on his thighs. 'So, there's no doubting Massimo sent you, but we need to extract a little information before we send you down to the sea bed with your pal.'

The man narrowed his eyes, looking from Phoenix's face to mine.

'Why would I tell you anything when you'll kill me anyway?' He spat the words at us.

Phoenix grinned, his scarred lips looking terrifying with the unhinged look in his eyes. He'd warned me he was going to intimidate our captive, and that I could stay inside rather than see it. I'd wanted to stay, but I hadn't realised how creepy Phoenix could be when he wanted to.

'Because,' Phoenix said, walking over to the chair where the man was bound, 'it's the difference between the state you go down to visit Davy Jones's locker. In one piece, neatly put down like a beloved pet. Or looking like a fucking smashed watermelon.'

A dark patch spread around the man's crotch, making Phoenix take a measured step backward.

'Just kill me already,' the man begged.

'All in good time. Now how about you tell me about Massimo's current whereabouts?' I wrapped my arms around myself as Phoenix spoke, wishing it was all over.

'I don't fucking know.' In a fit of rage, the man tore at the ropes, his chair shuddering against the deck, but holding him fast despite his outburst.

'Let's see if we can jog your memory,' Phoenix said with a smile. He opened a red case, pulling out what looked like an orange gun. The upper part of the case held white and orange tubes. He looked over at me, his face softening. 'You sure you want to be here?'

My stomach churned, but I gave a nod.

The gun opened up, and Phoenix slid one of the smaller, chunkier red tubes into the barrel-like portion.

'What the fuck do you think those are going to do? Sending for the fucking coastguard?' The man scoffed.

Phoenix stood, stretching out his back and clicking the barrel into place. 'It'll send for something...'

The man practically snarled when Phoenix walked over to him, pulling up his t-shirt to expose the man's stomach.

'A flare gun isn't going to do jack shit. You've got my fucking gun, why not just do the job properly?' I couldn't believe the guy had the balls to talk to Phoenix like that given his predicament. What an idiot.

A click sounded over the wind as Phoenix primed what I now knew to be the flare gun. I pressed my lips together, also not entirely convinced it would do much. Flares were just lights.

'Where were you supposed to take Laura?' Phoenix said, his voice lowering to a deep, almost intoxicating level.

'Fuck you.'

The shot gave more of a wet thunk than anything else. It took a moment for the man's face to register what happened. His eyes widened and he let out an ear-splitting yell. Blood trickled out of the wound on his lower abdomen, along with smoke.

'Holy fuck,' the man cried, his body writhing as if possessed by a whole army of demons. 'Make it stop. Make it fucking stop. It's burning my insides.'

A wave of vomit hit the back of my throat, and I squeezed my eyes shut, swallowing it down. The sounds escaping the man blackened my soul, horrible animalistic noises. Panting, crying, begging.

'Make it stop,' I pleaded after a minute.

'Soon,' Phoenix answered, gripping the man's hair and hauling his head back. 'Where were you supposed to meet? I need the details.'

'A warehouse in Sherbourne Wharf,' the injured man panted. 'Need to text the code to the number for when.'

We'd already secured the man's phone.

'What is the code?' Phoenix asked. Placing the gun against the man's chest when he hesitated.

'R-r-rabbit... for... dinner,' he stuttered. 'Send it to the one marked Graham.'

Phoenix stood back, taking the phone from his pocket, leaning forward to use the mans thumb to unlock it. He scrolled through, before typing for a moment. We waited, the man blubbering in his chair, foamy blood gushing from his stomach with every laboured breath.

The phone chimed, and Phoenix grinned. 'At least he's learned not to lie.'

Phoenix slid the phone back into his pocket before grabbing a set of shears from the ledge next to the seat where he'd placed the flare gun. He wrestled it around the man's thumb.

'You said you'd put me out of my misery,' the man said, his whole body shuddering.

'I will. But I'll need this, for the phone.'

A sickening crunch filled my ears moments before another sorrowful wail filled the air. The thumb hit the deck, rolling toward me as the boat lurched.

I wanted to puke, real fucking bad.

'Catch it,' Phoenix said, dropping the shears, but too late to catch the rolling digit.

Leaning down, I stopped the bloody stump of a finger, scooping it up, my face twisting in horror.

'Good girl,' Phoenix said, his face breaking into a smile.

I shuddered, closing my hand around the thumb and trying desperately to imagine it to be anything else. Another wave of vomit threatened me, and I struggled to fight it down.

With the flare gun back in hand, Phoenix stood behind the man, hauling his head roughly back. He forced the flare gun into the man's mouth, right down past his teeth.

'Next life, try to pick the right sides,' he said gruffly.

Tears slid down the man's face, blood bubbling from his stomach with each tortured breath. Phoenix cocked the flare gun, and my knees turned to jelly.

The man's body stiffened as the gun went off, his eyes bugging out of his head. Phoenix let go of him, and I watched as blood and sparks came sputtering out of his gaping mouth. Smoke billowed from his maw, like a dragon had taken residence in his stomach.

Strangled cries hit me, before foamy blood poured from his mouth like lava.

He thrashed, his arms cutting against the ropes, tearing through his own flesh as he burned up from the inside out.

I'd seen all I could take.

Running into the cabin, I tossed the thumb in the sink and ran down to the bedroom, burying myself beneath the duvet.

Killing was wrong.

So why did I feel so proud that Phoenix had tortured the man to protect me?

Why did I love that he killed the men who dared touch me?

I should have been disgusted. Terrified.

The sight of the man dying had horrified me, but it had also left me feeling something else.

Cherished.

FORTY

Phoenix

The bloody pony came running as soon as Laura set foot on shore, practically bowling her over in his eagerness to be loved upon.

The sweep of jealousy was less than before, but still there until he trotted over to me and stuffed that warm nose of his into my stomach.

'Okay, okay,' I laughed. He snorted at the sound of my voice. 'Yeah, we've made some adjustments since last time we met.'

Laura pulled a big shiny apple from the bag and pressed it to his mouth, holding it while he took big toothy bites.

I placed a hand on her lower back, readying myself for what I knew I had to say.

'I don't want you to come with me,' I started, but she turned to face me, her eyes narrow.

'You are not leaving me here.'

'No, not here, I'll find a little B&B tucked away somewhere—'

'Absolutely fucking not.' Steam may as well have been billowing out of her ears. 'I'm not being left, not knowing whether Massimo has buried you somewhere and is coming for me.'

Her chest rose sharply as she spoke, Muffin taking a step back and looking at me like I was a twat. 'I've spent my entire life being told what to do. I'm done. I'm coming with you. More than that, I'm going to be the bait.'

Fear pierced my stomach. 'No.'

'Yes. We text that number back and say you are dead. I snagged one of their masks, the one without the brains splattered into it, and you'll pretend to be him. We say the other one went down in the struggle.'

'They're not going to let me walk in there masked...'

'They think you don't talk. Mimic the guy's voice and it should buy us enough time...'

I intended to just run in guns blazing. My plan hadn't gone further than getting Laura to safety and drenching myself in rivers of Massimo's blood.

'I can't risk it,' I admitted, grazing my fingers over her chin, her eyes pulling me into her.

'It's not just you anymore. It's *we*. *Us*. I don't want to go on alone. If we go down, we both go down. It's him or us, Phoenix.' Her words were full of emotion, her lower lip trembling at the end of her sentence. 'I'm not rotting in some B&B worrying about whether you are coming back to me. I've lost everyone once. Never again. I'd prefer to die by your side than mourn you.'

'I can't...' I whispered, brushing my mouth against her perfect lips.

'I love you, Phoenix. Don't leave me.'

Her words broke me. Shattered my resolve. Alone I'd have been able to do it my way, recklessly. With her there, I'd need to be far more measured. But she loved me.

It was a bittersweet admission. Fireworks filled my heart, and in equal measure, pain filled my stomach.

I finally had a reason to live.

And I might lose it all.

Sweeping her into my embrace, I kissed her with feverish abandon, pouring every drop of emotion into her. We were both breathless when we broke our mouths apart.

'I need to show you before we leave,' she whispered against my neck.

'Show me what?'

'How much I need you to survive.'

She led me by the hand over the soft grass and to the cliff top looking out over the sea.

With tortured kisses, she pulled me down into the cold grass, her hands driving heat into every part of me she touched. Soft moans and desperate whimpers had me enthralled in every breath she took.

Without a clear reason how, she had us both naked beneath the orange hued sky, our limbs entangled in a sweet knot.

We'd fucked, but never had anyone touched me with such reverence. Every stroke of her lips infused my skin with adoration, and I returned her touches with impassioned pleas of my own.

Finally I understood the difference between fucking and

making love. Each motion of our sweat slicked bodies cried out our love to the world around us, our panting breaths like smoke signals dispersing into the universe, alerting all to our need for one another.

When she took me between her thighs, her lips spelled out lust filled incantations along my neck. I pulled her face to mine, devouring her sweet sighs as pleasure blossomed from every part of me she touched.

'He can't take this,' she moaned between feverish kisses. 'He can never take this.'

Tears pricked at the corners of my eyes as I lost myself in her soft body, feeling her wrap her love around me. It was a feeling I'd been missing since childhood, and it both mended me and broke me afresh.

'I'll love you until the rivers run dry,' I moaned against her lips. 'Until the stars perish and the moon ceases to rise. Until the world can no longer sustain our souls.'

Her cheeks were wet as she came apart beneath me, her orgasm slow and tortured, her tears flowing when I let go and gave her my everything. My cum spilled as freely as the tears dashing my cheeks.

All the anger I'd stored up since that fateful day which had stolen my future came running out of me. It filled her womb, and splashed her cheeks. I poured it into her mouth as I swallowed down her own needy sobs.

We watered the earth with our bodies, giving a plea out to the universe. Our love was worth saving.

If anyone was looking down over us, I only hoped they'd find us worthy of survival.

If not I'd spend whatever lives I moved onto searching for my perfect burning ember.

Waiting for her to set my world alight once again.

FORTY-ONE

Laura

The dingy motel down the street from the industrial estrange reeked of decades old cigarette smoke and body odour.

I sat gingerly on the end of the bed, clinging to the attackers phone, glad to have managed to change the password so we didn't need to carry a rotting thumb all the way down to Birmingham with us.

Phoenix stood by the window, peering through a crack in the curtains. He'd already cased out the warehouse ahead of the meeting. From what he could see, there were four men posted on the outside, two at each entrance. Massimo clearly had believed the ruse, to have so few men guarding the place.

Albeit, he would have his personal henchmen with him when he arrived, no doubt.

The phone buzzed in my lap, making my fingers light up where they clenched the screen.

> Hope you had fun last night breaking her in. Get her cleaned up. I want her to look fit for being my fiancée.

The previous night, when we'd awaited more instructions, Massimo had informed the remaining bounty hunter he could use me as a reward. It made me sick to my stomach. Phoenix had pretended to be the man, mimicking his voice while also crackling a packet near the receiver to make the signal appear disjointed. The veins in his neck had protruded as he fought to stay calm, fighting the urge to tear Massimo a new one over the phone.

It was all becoming very real.

Less than one hour until show time.

'There's his car,' Phoenix said, holding the binoculars up to his eyes and moving them faintly in line with what must have been the car.

My stomach knotted. In just over an hour I could be free.

Or dead.

'He's only brought two guys. They're big, and armed. With pistols at least.'

I gulped down the lump in my throat, the phone trembling in my hands.

Phoenix watched them for a few more minutes, until they walked into the warehouse.

'They used the south entrance, I imagine they'll have us use the same one.'

'What if he recognises you?' I asked.

'He's bound to see the differences between the dead guy and I, we won't have much time. You have the syringes?' He asked, trying to focus me back onto the task.

I nodded. Three syringes were fixed into the belt of my dress, hopefully small enough that I'd get past a brief pat down if they inflicted one.

'Just stick one in anyone who grabs you if things take a turn. I have the gun and ammo, I'll deal with the others.'

The plan was as simple as it was risky. Take out the four outside, the second two only after they'd given a call through to Massimo, assuming they had one at all. Then as soon as we got close enough, let Massimo grab me. While he was tied up with me, Phoenix would kill the other two. We needed to catch them by surprise for any chance at not having our brains blown out.

Minutes ticked by, my palms growing sweatier by the second.

Phoenix came and sat beside me, slipping one scarred hand into my palm. A gentle squeeze made me smile.

'Remember what I told you?' He asked.

'Bite off more than you can chew, and then chew like fuck?' The saying was stupid, but I could see what he meant. It was all or nothing. We went down guns blazing, or we won. No in between.

'Don't forget for a moment that I adore you,' Phoenix whispered, his mouth closing the gap between us and tracing his words against my neck.

The phone buzzed again, Massimo's words flashing up on the screen. 'Time to hand over the goods.'

I chewed on my bottom lip before looking up at Phoenix. He reached over to the table and grabbed the stolen mask.

'I could still go on my own...' he said, nerves evident in the timber of his voice now that the time to put our plan into action was upon us.

'No.' I pushed a steel I didn't fully believe into my voice. 'Time to chew like fuck, Phoenix.'

Feeling like we were walking toward our own execution, I pulled my shoulders back and smoothed my hair over my shoulder. The dress was new, cinching me in at the waist which only made my ass and bust seem even larger. Phoenix had assured me it would leave mouths hanging. I'd spent so many weeks in nothing but shorts and T-shirts that I felt like I was reviving some long dead version of me.

Every step made my knees wobble, whether from my stilettos or the fear, I didn't know.

I looked the part. Every bit a potential mafia wife.

I was hoping Massimo underestimated the true part of it that he'd overlooked.

Those women were fucking deadly.

FORTY-TWO

Phoenix

The two men at the rear of the warehouse were too easy to dispatch. I thought a man like Massimo would be less sloppy. They were distracted watching fucking football gathered around one of their phones. I'd crept up on them right as the commentator started speaking at a head-achingly quick pace, excitement in the tinny voice.

They never got to see the goal.

I wiped the knife off on one of their jackets, tucking it back into the sleeve of my jumper, it's switchblade once again concealed.

Thank god for the black clothing. The edge of my sleeve was sodden with warm blood, invisible in the dark alley, at least.

I dragged the bodies to the rear of a dumpster before nodding at Laura. I took her arm roughly in my hand, manhandling her round to the main entrance of the warehouse. She teetered on ridiculous heels, and two sets of eyes greeted us as big as saucers.

'Well, shit, no wonder the boss man wanted her back.' One said, nudging the other.

'Shame about the scar on her tit.' The other nodded toward the now healed bullet wound. 'Still, the tits are fuckable at least.'

Don't react.

Laura let out a pitiful squeal in front of me. 'Please, you've got to get me to Massimo. He's done horrible things to me...'

The men laughed. 'As if the boss man didn't sanction it. No one touched his goods without permission.'

The other chimed in, 'Damn I hope he's feeling generous again tonight, I'd give her something to complain about alright.'

'I'm just here to drop her off and pick up payment. Can we get on with it?' I feigned boredom despite the bulging anger feasting upon my every vein.

'Yeah mate, sorry.' The one on the right took his phone from his pocket. 'Yeah, they're here. I'll let 'em in. Course I'll check for weapons.'

The tone in his voice told me he wasn't talking directly to Massimo, he'd never have let the thinly veiled disdain fly.

'Pete'll check you both down before you go in, and you'll have to lose the mask. You look ridiculous.' The one with the phone said, gesturing at the other.

I pushed Laura towards Pete, his grinning making me want to punch out both of his eyes. The minute Laura was in front of him, he took full advantage of feeling her up, sliding his hand up her skirt while the other groped her backside.

She reached for one of the syringes.

'God, he's like a fucking virgin,' I said to the other, who guffawed loudly.

It was all the distraction I needed. Unsheathing my knife, I took a step closer while he looked over at Laura's hiked up dress. His eyes lingered for too long... and it was the last thing he saw. I thrust my blade through his throat, covering his mouth. Simultaneously, Laura thrust the needle into her victim's neck, his eyes widening and his mouth gaping like a fish. Moments later, he slumped to the floor, his heart stopping near instantly.

Laura stepped back, smoothing her skirt.

'You alright?' I asked, gently touching the small of her back after wiping my bloodied gloves on my victim's slumped form.

'Yeah,' she answered, breathy, her voice quavering a little.

'Ready for this?' I asked, kissing the back of her neck.

'No, you?'

'No. I think you should stay outside.'

'I can't,' she said. 'They'd open fire on you the minute you walked through that door without me.'

'They might not...'

'It's not a chance I'm willing to take. Just promise me you'll kill the fucker.' Her voice took on a new harshness I hadn't heard before. A layer of iron replenishing my own steel.

How could I promise that I'd save her? The last time I'd promised that... May's melting face flashed into my head. Hazy from the years without her, but horrid enough to rattle me.

I couldn't make promises I couldn't keep.

'I promise I'll kill him,' I whispered before capturing her lips for one last kiss.

I'd just have to make sure I kept the fucking promise.

The chill in the air was more than just temperature when we entered the room.

My fingers dug a touch too hard into the warm skin of Laura's arm, reluctant to let her out of my grip for even one moment.

Massimo stood from where he leaned against one wall of the warehouse room we entered. His two heavies flanked him, only a step or two behind. I needed to get as close as possible without my identity being revealed.

Massimo's eyes darkened when his gaze fell over Laura's tight fitting dress.

'Well, well, well. My little wife-to-be has finally returned.' He moved with an almost serpent like grace, his eyes unblinking as they drank up my girl.

'Hope you brought the cash,' I said, mimicking the bounty guy's voice the best I could.

'All in good time,' Massimo said, waving me off like a pestering child.

'Massimo,' Laura said bluntly. 'I should thank you for taking me away from that monster, but seeing as you left me for dead last time we met, I'll not be quick to fall to my knees.'

Massimo's face cracked into what some might say

resembled a smile. More like a devilish sneer. 'Let bygones be bygones. I cleaned up the problem of your hateful little family for you, didn't I?'

Laura pulled her arm from my grip, walking toward Massimo looking far more self assured than I felt.

'You killed my family,' she said, anger tingling the words.

Massimo gave a shrug, his gaze fixated on the swaying of her hips, the clip of her heels ricocheting around the hollow building.

Huge machinery surrounded us, oversized chains and big hulking wheels. Must have been some kind of construction storage building. One of the bodyguards stood with his hand on the gun at his waist, the shadow of one of the huge machines casting over him.

I'd have to take two of them out in quick succession if we stood half of a chance. Which meant leaving Laura to distract Massimo.

'I did you a favour,' Massimo said at last, 'you were just a pawn for them. A bargaining chip. Not even the first one, your brother was offered up first in the hopes I wanted a right hand man.'

Laura's shoulders tightened and I made a fist at my side.

'So what now? You pay off the guy and then what? You finish the job you failed at last time?' Laura's voice grew more shrill as anger flowed into her words.

'That's up to you.' Massimo closed the space between them, his fingers reaching out to caress Laura's jaw. 'I've had a little change of heart in the time you've been missing. I've fucked my way through half of the mafia princesses on offer, and they are all so fucking dull. But you, well you're scrappy. A survivor.'

The guards were listening to Massimo, watching as his fingers glided down to Laura's chest, circling the scar he'd left on her.

'See, branded as mine.'

I took the moment's distraction to take the bounty hunters gun from my waist, cocking it in one smooth motion. The first guards head exploded like a fucking over ripe watermelon, but the second was quick to react, throwing himself against the machine. The bullet meant for his head clipped his neck, sending a spray of blood arching over Laura's torso. I hoped it was enough to kill him.

Massimo grabbed Laura, turning her and putting his own gun to her temple.

'What's this now?' He said, excitement filling his voice. 'Did you mean to double cross me Laura?'

Laura quaked in his grip, one of his hands around her throat while the other pressed the muzzle of the gun to her head.

Fuck.

I kept my gun pointed at him, my heartbeat thundering in my ears.

'May as well take off the mask,' Massimo said. When I didn't comply he pulled back the gun before crashing it against Laura's skull hard enough for a trickle of blood to mar her pretty skin. 'Throw the gun down while you're at it.'

Rage flooded me, clouding my vision as I held steady, knowing that rushing him would just end with either Laura or me dead. He was still under the impression he had back up outside, and I wanted him not to take any chances.

Reaching up, I tore the mask off, tossing it on the floor.

'Hideous,' Massimo quipped with a mock shudder. 'Oh

Laura, don't tell me you bedded that monster. And you think you could come here and win your freedom? There's no freedom for you. You'll live your life under my fist, or you'll be underground next to the worms.'

Laura swallowed hard, her big eyes focussed on me.

'So what do you say my sweet, wear my ring and live as my pampered bitch, or die lusting for a scarred freak? I'm giving you a second chance at the life you always dreamed about. Yachts, parties, friends who envy you. Carrying my babies until they're old enough for a nanny, then spending your days by my side. You can have everything you always wanted.' Massimo's voice took on a sickly sweet undertone, and Laura's eyes glazed, before she inclined her head toward Massimo.

'You really want me?' She whispered, her voice packed full of wistfulness.

My heart broke.

But why would she want someone like me, when she could have someone who could offer her the world. All I'd offered was a pony who loved her anyway and my undying devotion.

I'd been a fool to believe it was enough.

She'd tricked me for her freedom.

'Of course I want to marry you,' she said, her face breaking into a sunny smile. 'It's all I ever wanted.'

'I know. It's all any woman wants.'

Massimo looked me up and down and shook his head. 'You believed she wanted you? That a woman like her could settle for a man with a face like a melted jack-o-lantern?'

Massimo's grip loosened slightly on Laura, and she grazed one hand over the hand he used to secure her throat, threading her fingers through it and dragging it to her lips. She placed a sweet kiss on his knuckles, looking up at him with rapt desire.

Desire she'd given to me.

I cocked my gun, aiming for Massimo's head.

'Watch your aim, Phoenix. One slip and you'll hit Laura. Looking at your face, I think that would kill you worse than I ever could.'

'She doesn't want you.' My words were hoarse, filled with anger.

'I should put him down,' Massimo said, his non-gun hand dropping down to Laura's side, gripping at her hip. 'Like the damaged dog he is.'

Laura simply shrugged.

'If you wish.'

It was death by a thousand fucking cuts.

FORTY-THREE

Laura

My palm was sweaty as I reached for a syringe, trying not to alert Massimo to my movements.

Phoenix's tortured face killed me. None of it was true, but I needed Massimo to believe me long enough to stick the damn needle into him.

Phoenix cocked his gun, taking aim, but Massimo was ready. He fired two shots, hitting Phoenix right in the torso. I screamed, trying to break free of Massimo. Phoenix's body hit the floor, his legs crumpling beneath him.

My soul all but ripped from my body, rage filling me and exploding from every fucking pore.

'No,' I screamed, grabbing the syringe from the back of my dress and turning, aiming it right for Massimo's bollocks.

He caught my wrist, crushing the bones in it, sending horrific pain radiating up my arm. The syringe fell to the floor, useless.

Massimo lifted one perfectly polished shoe and crushed

the syringe, its paralysing liquid seeping away into the concrete.

'Oh Laura,' Massimo tutted, pulling my body flush with his. He reached around my back, finding the final syringe and tossing it to the floor. The crunch a moment later stole away the last of my hope. 'You could have had it all, and you threw it away for what? An ugly loner?'

'He's more man that you could ever be,' I spat at him, all pretence gone. Phoenix died thinking I had turned my back on us, and I'd go down taking as much of Massimo to the grave as I could.

Lashing out with my teeth and nails, I scratched at him like a cornered animal, taking chunks of flesh from him under my nails. Letting all the anger and torment slide out of me in an outpouring of pure rage.

'You stupid fucking bitch,' he said, slapping me so hard across the face it left me seeing stars. 'Just like your useless fucking family. I've never been so glad to have removed people from my world.'

Using his pistol, he whipped me across the face, an explosion of pain filling my head. I stumbled and fell backwards, landing hard on the cold concrete. One of the machines loomed over us, and I tried to shimmy back between its wheels. My body ached, feeling broken in a hundred places. Tears stung my eyes. For the pain. For the loss. For Massimo winning.

It wasn't fair.

'Don't cry Laura, I'll make you come over my cock before I blow your brains out. You'll get to know what a real man feels like before you die.'

'If you were the last man on earth I wouldn't fuck you,' I said, my voice quavering.

'I'm not giving you a choice in the matter, sweetie.'

Flailing my legs, I fought him off as he neared me, but he hit me with the gun again, dazing me. I tried to pull myself up and failed. I had nothing left to give.

It had all been pointless. My whole life had been nothing but a giant waste of time. Trying to fill other people's expectations. Expectations that had driven me into the arms of the one man who'd truly loved me as I was. Not for my connections, or my clothing. Not for what he could gain by my family name. I'd come to Phoenix with nothing, and he'd made me feel like the wealthiest woman in the world.

I closed my eyes as Massimo kicked me, his sharp brogues inflicting yet more pain upon me. I let myself leave him. Leave the warehouse and find Phoenix back on the island. Back in the place I hoped to spend eternity.

'Come with me,' I whispered, seeing Phoenix's ghost appear over Massimo's shoulder. 'It's time to go.'

Two shots rang out above me, dull and tinny from my place in the fantasy world I'd escaped too.

'Not yet, my love.'

Not yet.

FORTY-FOUR

Phoenix

Massimo went down like a sack of shit.

His scream filled the warehouse, his gun clattering to the floor. In quick succession, I'd blown out both of his shoulders, the bullets tearing through flesh and bone–rendering his arms useless.

'You should have left us alone,' I sneered, grabbing the back of Massimo's suit jacket and dragging him toward the centre of the room. I couldn't tell if the animalistic noises he made were from pain or anger.

'She was mine first,' he choked out as I pushed him down onto his knees, pressing my gun against his forehead.

'You don't deserve a single moment of her time.' I pressed my finger against the trigger, grinning when Massimo trembled.

'Stop,' he begged, his arms hanging limply by his sides, darkness spreading through the material from his wounds. 'I can give you money. Or houses. Power. I have it all.'

A bead of sweat trickled down his forehead, glazing the barrel of my gun. 'You have nothing I want. There is only one thing I need, and she's already mine.'

When bribery failed, Massimo turned to rage. 'If you hurt me, my family will come after you and skin you both alive. My men will hunt you down.'

'They only do as you say out of fear. They have very little loyalty to you. The minute you cease to exist will bring nothing but relief to everyone who's ever known you. They'll sip champagne on your fucking grave.'

'Fuck you,' Massimo spat at me, launching himself against the floor and trying to move away from me. Without working arms, he looked like some kind of demented snake.

I sighed.

Aiming at the back of one kneecap, I squeezed the trigger. His cry filled the space, pleasure etching its way through my damaged body.

'There is no way out for you, Massimo. Your men are dead. No one is coming for you. I'm going to kill you, and then burn this place down with you inside. There won't be enough for your family to even identify you.'

'No,' he groaned, rolling on the floor, still trying to use his one good leg to push himself toward the door. 'Have mercy.'

'If there is anyone in this world who deserves no mercy, it's you. You've snatched power by hurting everyone you come into contact with. You don't see people, you see business deals and opportunities to further your own gain. You deserve far worse than I'm going to give you.'

Massimo struggled feebly as I put my gun down and hauled him up, my face inches from his.

'I'm doing this for Laura.'

I walked him backwards, half dragging him with his mangled leg. A large metal hook hung directly behind him, and with one great push, I pressed us both into it. A wet crunch gave way to a pained yell as the hook ate into his muscles.

His eyes widened, tears and snot dripping, a desperate choking sound coming from him.

'That's for all the hurt you've caused her,' I growled.

Leaving him struggling on the hook, I moved to the vehicle, turning the keys left in the ignition and smiling as the engine kicked into gear. The chain attached to the hook creaked when I hit the button to wind it in.

His wails grew more panicked when his feet suspended above the floor, his body jerking and only making the hook bite further into his sinew.

I stopped the machine when his feet were at my eye level.

'Get me down,' he croaked when I neared.

Not a chance.

'Before you die, you are going to know what it's like to burn.'

He kicked with his one working leg, and I laughed as I made my way to the edge of the room, grabbing one of the jerry-cans of petrol stashed there for the smaller vehicles.

I splashed it liberally over his legs, knowing the flames would burn their way more slowly up his body if I kept the splashes there alone.

'Phoenix, please, no. Just shoot me!'

Standing back, I lit a match, delighting in the way his eyes widened.

'Goodbye, Massimo,' I said, flicking the lit match at his feet.

With the flames engulfing his trousers, his manic flailing increased, the hook cutting into his intestines with every flinch.

To the crescendo of his screams, I went to fetch my girl.

FORTY-FIVE

Laura

Gentle arms lifted me, my head lolling against a wide chest. The black material was warm and wet against my cheek, a coppery twang invading my senses. Pain filled my body, leaving my limbs weak and useless.

Opening my eyes proved difficult, barely a slice of vision available. My headache intensified as I looked over a broad shoulder.

'Don't look,' Phoenix said softly.

But I wanted to look.

I'd blacked out, and I needed to see for myself that Massimo was truly dead.

Orange flames hungrily consumed Massimo. Massimo's limp form dangled in the middle of the room, the giant hook protruding through his back. His face gawped like a dead fish, guts spilling out through the large hole left from the hook impaling him.

His body turned slowly above the greedy flames, roasting the devil. It was like watching hell welcome him.

Relief swept through me, leaving me sobbing against Phoenix.

'I didn't mean any of it,' I whispered, keeping my eyes on Massimo as the flames grasped at him.

'I know, I heard you after.' Phoenix stroked a thumb over my thigh, right where his arms supported me.

'He's really dead?' I asked.

'One hundred percent. The fucker's gone.'

'Thank you.' My words came out pained, and I finally dragged my eyes from Massimo as we left the room. 'I thought you were dead, too.'

'Not this time,' he assured me, his breath crackled in his chest.

'We need to get to a hospital,' I murmured, my vision blurring as we stepped out into the night.

The cold night air greeted us, in the distance a siren wailed.

'Later, I need to get us out of here,' Phoenix said, his voice soothing. His motorbike sat around the corner, and he fixed a helmet over both of our heads. I winced as he settled me over the seat and climbed on behind me.

'It's going to hurt, but we need to put some distance between us and the building.'

I nodded, shivering as he wrapped his arms around me.

'I love you,' I whispered into the interior of my helmet, my head swimming with the increased pain as he kicked the bike into gear.

I could have sworn I heard *I love you* drifting on the air right back to me.

Pain took over as we moved, my entire focus taken by trying not to vomit. My balance was off, my ability to grip the bike with my injured legs impaired.

We limped our way back toward Scotland.

Toward home.

FORTY-SIX

Phoenix

Making it to the boat wasn't an option. I'd moored it too far from the border.

Car lights streaked past me as I pulled off of the motorway, my vision blurring with each passing mile.

Laura sagged against me, her body floppy but her chest still rising.

My blood loss was peaking, and I couldn't drive for much longer. Every breath pained me, and I needed to see Laura in safe hands before I gave into the jaws of death that snapped at my heels.

The McGowans'.

Their mansion was on the outskirts of the city, not too far from our location. I'd helped them out on occasion, and hoped they wouldn't just leave us to rot.

The bike slid on the road, rocking and swerving as I neared the elaborate gates which blocked the entry.

My gloved hands left a bloody print on the buzzer, my bodyweight leaning too hard as I pressed it.

'Hello?' a female voice crackled over the tannoy.

'It's Phoenix. We need help.' Even talking had become difficult. Between holding Laura on the bike, and my own ailing consciousness, I couldn't take any more. I just had to see her to safety.

The McGowans' were a crime family, but ones with somewhat of a conscience at least.

'Please?' I begged, my breath feeling wetter with every inhale.

Silence greeted me.

I pressed my helmet against the back of Laura's, wishing that the plastic didn't separate us. If I were to die on the spot, I wished to inhale her scent one final time.

With a creak, the gate swung open.

The bike juddered beneath me, my control of it slipping. Sleep beckoned me with her sweet embrace, enticing me away from the pain and hardship.

Nearly there, I told myself. *Just get Laura to the door.*

Gravel crunched beneath my wheels as we neared the mansion. The ornate wooden door stood open, a female figure blocking the yellow glow from within.

So close.

The bike skidded out from under us, our glacial speed causing it to topple us from the seat. The ground met me with a final, desperate bite before I gave in to the call of nothingness.

Laura, I whispered as footsteps sounded beyond the darkness. *Save Laura.*

FORTY-SEVEN

Laura

Serenity surrounded me. The bed beneath me was cloud-like, the air filled with a warm spiced scent.

Awareness came to me slowly, filtering into my senses piece by piece. An ache filled my arm as I tried to move, another biting at my head when I struggled to open my eyes.

The light hurt, and my left eye was stuck closed. The room came into focus when I forced my right eye open. My arm lay, bandaged, on an unfamiliar bed, bruises and butterfly-stitched cuts snaking over my skin.

Realisation hit me like a freight train, jolting me upright and causing me to wince.

'Phoenix?' I called out, pulling myself to my feet. My left leg couldn't take my full weight, and I limped toward the door.

Was I in a hospital? It was too fancy. Too ornate.

'Phoenix,' I choked out, pushing open the door and tumbling into the hallway.

Silence awaited. Limping, I dragged myself toward another door, opening it to find a similar room to the one I'd awoken in.

Empty.

I kept going, finding myself at the top of a grand staircase, leading down into an open library. I teetered at the top of the stairs, the floor zooming up toward my face.

'Whoa, easy,' a man's voice said, firm hands gripping around my upper arms.

'Where is he?' I begged, my legs jellying. The man smelled expensive, a deep spice-filled scent enveloping me as he wrapped sturdy arms around my waist and supported me. 'Is he dead? He can't be dead...'

'He's okay, I'll take you to him. I'm Ewen.' He turned me from the stairs, and guided me with a firm grip around my waist. 'You've been out of it for a few days, but you'll both live.'

'Thank you,' I said, grimacing as pain radiated through my hip.

'I'm not the only person who owes Phoenix one for killing that fucker Massimo, he had a long list of enemies. Glad you guys made it here, it was a close call.' Ewen stopped at a door, knocking softly before nudging it open.

Phoenix was paler than I'd seen him, his top missing and his chest a patchwork of bandages.

The moment I laid eyes on him, a sob ripped from my mouth, and momentarily pain ceased to exist.

Crossing the room, I threw myself on the bed, wrapping my arms around him.

'There you are,' he whispered, his fingers cradling the back of my neck as I adorned his chest with my tears.

'I thought…' I murmured, pushing my hand over his heart to assure myself of its steady beat.

'Shh,' he crooned, giving Ewen a crooked smile over my shoulder. He backed out of the room, leaving us to each other. 'It's over. We did it. You don't need to hide anymore.'

I finally let relief sweep over me. After all of the hurt and the fear and the loss, I could finally relax. 'It's over.'

'And just beginning,' Phoenix said, pulling me gently to his mouth and pressing a tender kiss to me. 'Assuming you want to stay with me?'

A smile covered my face. 'What are you offering?'

'Not much. The ruins of a cottage, a mangy old pony, more grass than you could hope to cut in a lifetime.' He whispered the words against my lips, and I grinned.

'It's a tempting offer…'

'I'll sweeten the pot,' he added, his fingers sinking into the hair at the back of my head. 'I can make you come on my tongue until you see the stars. I will spend every single day working to build us a home, and every night between your thighs building a family with you. I'll cherish every second you offer me, until the minute my useless heart packs in.'

Warmth flooded me at his sweet words, and I pressed my lips to his, greedily stealing a deep kiss. He winced, but held me firmly to him, his tongue siding over mine.

'You might have to wait just a little longer for me to fulfil the promises though, I feel like I've been hit by a bus.' Phoenix gave a chuckle, and I slid down, tucking myself neatly into the space between his arm and his chest.

'I've got all the time in the world.'

EPILOGUE

Phoenix

My arm shuddered as I hammered the long nails into the post. Sweat trickled down my spine in the warm summer air, a rare enough feat in Scotland.

The stables were almost complete, built to Laura's specification. No gates, it needed to be open to the ponies, so they could come and go as they pleased.

Months had passed since our encounter with Massimo, and life on the island was sweet. I'd handed over a load of money to have the new cottage built as quickly as possible, needing us to have a place to settle into together. To begin our new chapter.

The builders were finally gone, leaving us to indulge in one another without any witnesses.

The days were short, and the nights long, and with each passing day, I only fell deeper in love with Laura. Without her family's expectations, she flourished. She'd pulled me well into civilisation, getting our house fitted with satellite internet and a big assed TV. She'd also enrolled into multiple courses that interested her, cooking in Paris, sculpting in Italy and even writing at a little retreat in Cornwall. I'd gladly fly her to the ends of the earth to indulge any whim which took her.

Laura swiped her paint brush over the fence, using wood paint to weather seal the parts I'd finished. She'd piled her hair up on top of her head, and had on a pair of loose dungarees. Freckles smattered her nose where the sun had danced upon her cheeks.

The sight of her made my chest clench, even after the many months we'd spent together.

She shooed a chicken out of the way, laughing as it pecked at her shoes.

'Maggie,' she laughed, waving her free hand above the chicken. 'Honestly, these chickens are the most unruly bunch yet.'

'Maybe we need a bigger hen house?' I said.

'I think she just wants to get into the veggie patch, she's a bugger for going at the lettuce.' Laura pasted more paint onto the fence.

'I'll bugger your lettuce,' I joked, winking at Laura when she rolled her eyes.

'You can't bugger there anyway. That's an oxymoron.'

'How about I try?' I said, dropping the hammer and moving over to my girl, looping an arm around her waist.

'It's been a while…' she replied, her pupils dilating. She pressed her lips against my neck.

'I'm clearly failing my husbandly duties,' I murmured, 'If you need a good ass-fucking you need only ask…'

'I prefer it when you demand.'

My dirty girl.

I was halfway to hard already, tipping her head back and sinking my teeth into her neck, her pulse beating against my tongue.

'Not yet,' she moaned. She pulled away from me, putting the top on her paint can and wrapping foil around the wet end of the brush. 'I have a surprise for you first.'

Taking me by the hand, she led me toward the cottage, in through the open patio doors to the bright and spacious kitchen diner.

'What's this in aid of?' I asked.

Laura walked over to the pantry, before emerging with a decadent looking chocolate cake. 'Happy birthday, Phoenix.'

The world shuddered to a halt, throwing me back to the last time anyone had mentioned my birthday. I'd been in the hospital burns unit. The sweet nurses had brought me a cupcake and some new books. I cried for two days. From then on, I hadn't cared to remember. Every forgotten birthday one less ache. I'd never had anyone to care about them after my family had passed. My uncle certainly never cared to buy me a gift or wish me a happy birthday.

'How did you know it's my birthday?'

'I wanted to know. It's important. I need to be able to celebrate you, like you did on my birthday.' Laura placed the cake on the counter, pushing a handful of brightly coloured candles into the top. I watched as she lit each one. Warmth filled my stomach at the sweet gesture.

'Make a wish,' she said, gesturing to the cake.

I leaned down, blowing the candles out in one swift move. I didn't need to make a wish, I already had everything I needed.

'Thank you.' I moved around the counter to pull her into my arms.

'Wait, one more thing.' She practically skipped over to a drawer, and pulled out a garishly wrapped gift, the most colourful paper I'd ever seen. Joy pierced me at the giddiness in her eyes.

'I hope you like it,' she muttered, pushing it into my hands.

The taped corners came away in my fingers, revealing a photo frame. The world ceased to turn for a moment as I stared at the picture in my hands. My eyes grew glassy as I pressed my fingers to the glass, running them over their faces.

The four of us were there, cuddled together, wind in our hair and smiles plastered over our faces. Mum's arm was outstretched, holding the camera. It threw me right back to the day by the seaside, we'd eaten sandwiches on the shore, picking errant bits of sand from their edges. May and I had run from the waves, our laughter filling the air despite the cold and windy day.

Laura had given me more than just a photo. She'd given me their faces back. They'd blurred over time, the details becoming foggy. And sweet little May. Her intact cheeks, the bright, silly smile. Safe. Happy.

Fuck. My fingers shook and Laura wrapped hers around them, steadying me.

'It's perfect,' I whispered. 'How did you find it?'

'I hope you don't mind, but I looked up the accident. It's the image the papers were using. I traced it down, and there was a copy in an old box in their storage room.'

I couldn't stop staring, memorising every line of their faces.

'There's more. They had an address for a woman, your father's mother. I looked into it, and she's still alive. I have her number if you decide you'd like it.'

My brow creased. Until a vague picture of a woman clicked into place. Devon Granny. We'd only seen her sporadically, and I'd lost all contact when my Uncle took me off grid. She was still alive?

'You're amazing,' I whispered.

'You might even have more family. Cousins, aunts, uncles. I don't know for sure, but I'll stand right beside you if you want to meet them.' Laura took the picture and placed it onto the counter, wrapping her arms around my neck.

'I don't deserve you,' I whispered into her hair.

'But you're stuck with me anyway.'

Laura

'Is it just me, or is Muffin getting kind of fat?' I asked, looking at Muffin's widening stomach.

Phoenix looked up from the fire he was busy stoking, the ring of rocks containing it. He cocked his head before grinning.

'Did you ever check that Muffin was a boy?'

I stammered, had I ever checked? How had I even decided it was a he?

'I don't know.'

Phoenix let out a laugh, the fire glinting in his eyes. 'Seems like Muffin's been getting some stuffin'.'

'Phoenix,' I groaned, pushing against him. 'You think he... or she I guess... is having a baby?'

'Well, the wild ponies have been here forever, occasionally they do make a new one.'

Excitement filled me. A foal! We were going to have a foal.

'I hope your face is that excited when I put a baby in you,' Phoenix's voice dropped to a heated growl, his eyes darkening in the firelight. He reached over and grabbed a handful of rope. My insides flipped and I crossed my wrists over, holding them out.

'Are we starting now?' I asked, teasing him as he wrapped a loop of rope around my wrists.

'Doesn't hurt to practice.'

A sharp tug on the rope had me like putty in his hands. It had been a little while since we'd played like that, we were so lost in building and decorating that when we eventually crashed into bed it was all about satisfaction, not teasing.

'What are you going to do with me?' I asked, making my voice sound coy.

'I'm going to bend you over that fence and fuck some babies into your pretty cunt, my love.'

My body clenched in response to his heated words. While I wasn't quite ready for babies and the chaos they brought, I loved when he got all possessive, telling me he was going to put them in me anyway.

'I'm going to use you like a little pet ready to be bred, who will take my dick with a smile and a thank you.' Phoenix let out a little groan at the end of his sentence, pushing his hand up under my skirt and touching me with feral abandon.

'Yes, Sir,' I moaned, grinding myself against his skilled fingers.

His expression deepened at the word Sir, something feral filling his eyes.

Picking me up, he tossed me over his shoulder, the rope dragging at his feet as he stalked over to the fence.

Within seconds he had me over the rough wood, my hands tied to the bottom fence post on the opposite side to my legs.

Kicking my legs wide, he looped the rope around them too, restricting my movement entirely.

My hair fell over my face and I let out a needy moan when he lifted my dress and dragged my panties down as far as they'd go with the way my legs were splayed wide.

There was no warm up, no tenderness as he plunged two fingers deep inside me.

'Fuck,' I groaned, wanting to push back against him, needing more. The ropes held me utterly immobile.

'Trussed up like a farm animal ready to be bred. Shall I fill your pretty pink cunt with cum, my love?'

'Please?' I begged, feeling the way his fingers slid into me without any friction, I knew I was already sodden for him.

The sound of his zipper gave me butterflies, even after the months we'd spent together, I never got bored of him. He forever found ways to make my heart, and my pussy, flutter for him.

He removed his fingers, replacing them with the head of his cock. I trembled as I waited for that delightful first stretch around him.

'Phoenix,' I whined, trying to wriggle backwards when he made me wait.

'What happened to Sir?' He asked, landing one hard slap against my ass.

'Oh!' The sharp smack took my breath away, and that was the moment he gripped my hips and slid a tiny bit further into me. It was sheer bloody torture. He slid just enough to make me moan, but not enough to satisfy me.

'What's wrong Laura? Need more of this cock? Is your hungry little cunt so desperate to be filled?'

'Yes,' I whimpered. 'I need it.'

'I know you do.'

He slammed into me, ramming the breath right from my lungs. The sudden invasion made my legs quake, and I panted as he remained there, fully seated inside me, stretching me mercilessly.

'You look so delicious spread around my dick, your pussy lips all wet and gleaming and red with desire. This, right here, is the only place I ever need to be, cock deep in my girl.'

'Yes, Sir,' I moaned.

My hips rammed against the fence post as he fucked me in earnest, pulling out to the tip before sliding back home. Every deep thrust pulled a squeal from my lips at the harshness of the thrusts.

'A rough fuck is what my pet needs, isn't it? Not nice lovemaking. Bent over and taken like a proper little slut.'

'Yes!' I cried between thrusts, my voice practically a yelp.

'Always ready to take every inch. And once I'm done pumping you full of hot cum, I'll come around to the other side of the fence and let you wash your cunt off of me with your tongue before fucking you all over again. I wonder how many times I can fill you before the sunrises? How much you'll take for me.'

I'd take it all. Everything he had to give. Because despite his degrading words, I knew the depth of his adoration for me. Knew that before the sun rose he'd wring orgasm after sweet orgasm from my body. He'd make me see both the heavens and beg from the pits of hell, and after, he'd wrap me in his arms and show me his love.

His fingers found their way around my hips and to the centre of my pleasure, twisting and teasing along with the wild slap of his hips against my ass.

He pushed me over the edge, caressing an earth-shattering orgasm from me while filling me with ropes of hot cum. My cries filled the night air, his puffs of breath warming my back. His thrusts slowed until he slid out of me, his fingers rubbing idly against me until the last shudders of pleasure quaked.

Catching my breath, I waited as he walked around to the other side of the fence, crouching down beside me and capturing my lips in a harsh kiss.

'I fucking love the very arse off of you,' he whispered. 'You were such a good girl, took me ever so well.'

'I love you too,' I sighed, happiness filling my sex addled mind.

'We're not done yet though, are we?' Phoenix crooned.

I shook my head and opened my mouth, ready to drive him to the point where he'd need to fuck me again.

And again.

And again.

Forever more.

Printed in Great Britain
by Amazon